"Roberts' reimagining of these well-known biblical stories is nothing short of masterful. The stories are as bright and fantastical as they are dark and powerful. There is a profound humanness in these stories that invite you to reconsider your own place in a world fraught by groans of anguish and songs of hope."

—Michael Vazquez
founder of Brave Commons, an LGBTQ+ Christian advocacy organization

"Nathan Roberts is a gifted-storyteller, a writer of great imagination, and a brilliant biblical interpreter! These stories will provoke you to think deeply and consider the connections to twenty-first century life that he weaves through them."

—Karen Gonzalez
author of *The God Who Sees: Immigrants, the Bible, and the Journey to Belong*

"Deserted's reimagining of classic Bible stories without God as the centerpiece offers us a glimpse of the truest essence of the human condition when we only have to be accountable to ourselves and each other and not an almighty, judgmental God."

—Ulysses Burley III
founder of UBtheCURE, a faith, health, and human rights organization

"Ingeniously reworking some of the most familiar biblical tales. These men and women face recognizable moral dilemmas both large and small, striving to do what's right, and in the process, the Bible once more emerges as a living text that offers guidance in moments of doubt."

—Keith Harris
City Pages magazine

"If you have never met the characters in the Bible or if you have read about them a thousand times, I promise you will be drawn into Roberts' vivid, engaging, and artfully troubling retellings. With deft insight and good humor. Read this book to ignite your imagination."

—DEBBIE BLUE
author of *Consider the Women: A Provocative Guide to Three Matriarchs of the Bible*

"Reading these short stories sent me back to my Bible (and my farm roots) with fresh eyes on ancient stories of faith. While God is not an 'out loud' actor in these stories, they expand my imagination of God at work in the world."

—BONNIE WILCOX
Senior Pastor, First Lutheran Church, Columbia Heights, Minnesota

Deserted

Deserted

Retelling Bible Stories Without an Angry God

NATHAN ROBERTS

Illustrations by Alxndr Jones

RESOURCE *Publications* · Eugene, Oregon

DESERTED
Retelling Bible Stories Without an Angry God

Resource Publications
An Imprint of Wipf and Stock Publishers
199 W. 8th Ave., Suite 3
Eugene, OR 97401

www.wipfandstock.com

PAPERBACK ISBN: 978-1-5326-8228-5
HARDCOVER ISBN: 978-1-5326-8229-2
EBOOK ISBN: 978-1-5326-8230-8

Manufactured in the U.S.A.   JULY 17, 2019

Contents

Acknowledgments

I want to begin by thanking my wife, Emilie. Her continued love, support, inspiration, conversations, and hospitality make my writing, and my life, possible.

Thank you to Ben Barnhart for combing out the snarls in my sentences. To alxndr jones for making the illustrations so beautiful and profound. To the team at Wipf and Stock for believing in this book. To everyone who listened to me tell and retell these stories at the School House and over cups of coffee. To everyone who read and reread drafts of this book, especially Jeremiah, Rev. Lawrence, Rev. Bonnie, Luke, Gina, Andrew, Sarah, Jimmy, Michael, Rozella, Dr. Ulysses, Suzanne, Karen, and Keith. To Walter for giving me a chance to be on the radio. To Rev. Debbie, Rev. Russell, and the House of Mercy for introducing me to the Midrash and reteaching me to read the Bible. To my First Lutheran family, my Minneapolis UCC family, the Salt Collective writers, the Kimpurs, and my Kenyan family for so many wonderful years of reading the Bible in community together.

And finally to you. I sincerely appreciate you sharing your time with us, and I hope you continue to retell and rearrange these beautiful stories.

Introduction

I remember being a little kid and lying on the carpet as I stared at the pictures in the illustrated children's Bible while adults read me the stories about Moses and Pharoah, Noah, and Eve. The characters were all drawn as doe-eyed white people with washed hair and long, clean robes. They didn't look like the people who lived under a hot sun in the middle of the desert. They looked more like adults from my church playing dress-up. My Sunday School teacher had sang to us, *Father Abraham, had many sons. And I am one of them and so are you,* so I assumed pale skin was a family trait that went all the way back.

When I was in 3rd grade I was given my own copy of the *full* Bible, the *adult* Bible. I eagerly reread all my favorite stories and I found, much to my delight, that there were many salacious details that my picture Bible had conveniently omitted. There was sex and violence on practically every page. I was in possession of a book I would have never been allowed to read if it didn't have the word "Holy" on the cover. By the time I graduated high school, I had read the full Bible cover to cover four times.

It wasn't until my mid 20s that I began to read theses stories in the original Hebrew language. The stories felt very different. The verses in English had felt smooth and reliable. The tone and vocabulary was even and polished. But when I read these same verses in Hebrew, they felt stilted. The story of Noah and the ark bore the scars of being edited. The sentences had been broken and mended. The tone and phrasing shifted sometimes in the middle of a story.

As I reread Genesis it happened in story after story. The whole book of Genesis felt collaged together from different writers. All this had been polished over by the English translators.

I began to research. That's when I discovered the Source Theory. I learned that the stories I had grown up reading in the Bible, were actually retellings of stories. Hebrew fathers told their sons about Isaac and the goat as they wandered the hills in search of fresh grazing land. Mothers told their daughters about Eve and a talking snake around the cooking fire. These were family stories told and retold across the desert for hundreds of years. And like so many family stories, they changed and grew with each retelling.

Then around 1000 B.C. Hebrew priests in Jerusalem began collecting these stories, and for 500 years they filled scroll after scroll. Until 587 B.C. when Israel lost a long, brutal war with the Babylonian empire and the capital city of Jerusalem was destroyed. The Hebrew people were enslaved, children were separated from their parents, scrolls were burned, and for the first time Hebrew stories fell under threat of being lost and forgotten.

So the Hebrew priests decided to collect their people's stories, poems, and songs, and place them alongside laws and rituals. These enslaved priests become the editors of what we now know as the Hebrew Bible.

The original Hebrew text still bears the scars of their editing. Over the centuries different versions had emerged in different villages. And when there were two treasured versions of a story, the editors sometimes chose to catalog them side-by-side in the text. The starkest example of this is the two creation stories—the story of the all-powerful creator of the universe, placed beside the very emotional Yahweh walking next to Adam and Eve in a small garden. Sometimes they wove two versions together, as in the story of Noah and the ark. If you read closely you can see that everything happens twice. The animals are loaded on the ark twice, earth is flooded twice, Noah sends out a raven first, then a dove. And in the Hebrew these couplets make the text feel stilted. Broken and mended.

When I learned this, I felt, well, shocked. I felt lied to by the English translators and tricked by the pastors who told me over and over again that the Bible was a historical account. These stories were what *really* happened, they'd told me.

But it was around this same time that I met a village elder from the Pokot tribe of northern Kenya. Michael Kimpur grew up in a nomadic community. He herded cows and listened to his village elders retell stories around campfires. When I asked him if there was a written collection of the stories of his people, he told me something that changed my perspective on the Bible. "There are no official versions of our stories," he said. "It is the responsibility of the elders in each generation to retell these stories in a way that meets the needs of the next generation."

Shortly after this exchange, I was in the religion section of an old bookstore, my head tilted sideways reading book titles. I stumbled across a collection of Jewish folk retellings of Biblical stories called midrash. The collection contained wild and fantastic retellings that had been told and retold by rabbis over thousands of years. These rabbis played with the details. In one retelling of Adam and the garden, Adam is created as a giant, so big he can barely fit on the earth, his head reaches all the way to the stars. And when this oversized and overconfident Adam begins to question the judgment of the angels, he is shrunk down to normal human size. The story ends with Adam sleeping, dreaming of being a giant and walking among the stars.

In comic books they call these types of stories an *Elseworld* story. A story set in a world where things are just a little different. A great example of an *Elseworld* story is *Superman Red Son* by Mark Millar. In *Red Son* baby Superman's alien shuttle flies from the exploding planet of Krypton through space, but it doesn't land in the Kent family farm in Kansas. Instead, his shuttle lands in the Soviet Union on a collective farm with a Ukrainian family. Changing this one detail about Superman's story, changes so much.

Superman still has the power of flight and super strength. But he doesn't fight for "Truth, justice, and the American Way." Instead Superman is heralded on Soviet radio broadcasts "as the Champion of the common worker who fights a never-ending battle for Stalin, socialism, and the international expansion of the Warsaw Pact." And readers are suddenly faced with the harsh reality of how terrifying Superman's power is when he is working for Stalin.

Sometimes all it takes is changing one detail to see a familiar story in a whole new light.

The book you are holding is a collection of reimagined stories from Genesis and Exodus set in a Biblical *Elseworld.* If you grew up with Bible stories, I suspect the setting and characters will feel familiar, but I did change one little detail–in these stories the Hebrew God, Yahweh, doesn't exist. Why take Yahweh out of the Bible you ask? Because I wanted to see what would happen next.

I hope my stories inspire you to play with the Biblical details so that we can meet the needs of this and the next generation.

NATHAN ROBERTS

Adam gave names to all cattle, and to the birds of the air, and to every animal of the field, but for the man there was not found a helper as his partner.

—GENESIS 1:20

Cain and the Snake

"What should we name it?" Adam asked holding a small brown snake by the tail. His two young sons, Cain and Abel, watched as its scaly body wriggled back and forth, its red tongue flickering in and out like a sword.

"What about calling it a dirt snake?" Abel shouted, his four-year-old fingers petting the very end of the tail.

"Hm . . . dirt snake you say?" He smiled turning the snake as he rubbed his long graying beard.

"But remember that we found it on the *branch* of a tree?" Adam added.

"How about Branch Snake!" Abel shouted.

"Excellent idea!" Adam grinned, pulling out a long dusty scroll from his satchel.

"Is that the kind of snake that bit mommy?" Cain asked as he watched the snake slither with a sick feeling in his stomach. He stepped off the red dirt path onto a large rock, his eyes checking nearby branches and tree trunks.

They had walked all morning, up and down the shadowy forest trails, surrounded on all sides by chirping and squawking, the howls of hidden monkeys, and creatures rustling in the tall dark bushes. It had been a long time since he had gone exploring and the forest seemed to hold a lot more creatures than he had remembered. But the snake wriggling between his dad's fingers was the first animal Cain had actually seen.

"What was that about mommy?" Adam asked. His knees were in the dirt, a long scroll unrolled in front of him. Adam held the snake with one hand and sketched it with the other. The scroll was already covered in dozens of snake drawings each with its own new name.

"I said," Cain asked louder, "is that the kind of snake that bit mommy?" Cain could feel his heart beating faster. He rubbed the sweat off his forehead.

"No, no," Adam reassured his son, not bothering to look up from his drawing. "That snake was much *much* bigger."

"*Bigger?*" Cain whispered to himself as he checked the waist-high grass that lined the trail.

Abel's small frame leaned against his father's shoulder. "Hey, don't bump me while I'm drawing," Adam laughed and licked a finger to blot out a stray line jutting out of the branch snake like a leg. Adam finished drawing and rolled up the scroll. Then he gently placed the newly named branch snake back on a low-hanging naked branch.

"Don't worry, Cain," Adam smiled and lifted Abel onto his shoulders. "We've been walking these hills for months and we haven't seen anything to worry about." Adam reached out for Cain's hand, and Cain felt his sweaty palm swallowed in his father's rough skin. Secretly, Cain wished he was still small enough to ride on his father's shoulders.

The three of them walked until the trail abruptly ended at the edge of a steep, grassy hill. The long wet green shoots reached all the way up to Cain's belly button. The hill sizzled with the sounds of insects he didn't recognize. At the bottom Cain could see a small river bordered by trees. Cain hoped they were just stopping to look at the river.

"You can't see it from here, but the river is full of animals." Adam said, gently squeezing Cain's hand. "It's better up close."

"Way better." Abel smirked down at Cain from the safety of their dad's shoulders.

Cain's heart sank as his father gently edged off the trail and into the waist-high and very wet grass. His naked toes felt for scales as his eyes checked for bugs. He kept painfully stepping on stones with his bare feet, and his robe felt heavy and wet. The hill got steeper and he nearly fell a few times. But each time his dad's grip tightened before he hit the ground.

At the bottom of the hill Cain stepped out of the grass. His robe was soaking wet. After he was sure there were no insects on him, he looked at the river. It was definitely not better looking *up close*. It was just another muddy creek, basically the same as the one behind their house. It had a few big rocks that marked the fast-moving current and a few medium-sized trees. This was not worth spending the rest of the day in a soaking wet robe.

Then he saw a ripple near the shoreline. He watched it and wondered if he had imagined it. He stepped off the warm sand and up onto an exposed tree root. Then there was another ripple, this time above the water. Cain stared at two beady eyes and a long slimy snout. The rest of its massive body remained hidden just under the brown water.

"Snake!" Cain shouted. "There's a snake!" is eyes unable to look away from the wiggling slimey head. Then Cain froze, thinking maybe it wouldn't be able to see him if he didn't move.

It seemed to work. For a moment the head stopped, and then its mouth opened and a large tongue flopped out. Then two legs with long claws poked out of the water, followed by a large shell almost as big as Cain's whole body.

"You thought that was a snake?" Abel cackled from behind him.

Cain felt his face grow hot with embarrassment. He suddenly wished he was back at home, in his bed and under his blanket. He regretted ever agreeing to come on this hike, forgetting for the moment that he had actually begged to come along.

"Now, now Abel, cut that out." Adam said pinching Abel's leg. "That right there is a *very* big turtle," Adam whistled. "And it's better to be cautious. Turtles *can* bite."

Cain watched his dad pull out a scroll and his heart leaped. This was a new animal and he had discovered it. "Can we call it . . ." Cain paused, unable to think of a name.

"How about river turtle?" Abel shouted.

"Let's let Cain have a try. He found it," Adam said as he continued to sketch the turtle's large shell.

Cain watched the turtle relax its claws into the warm sand, its head lowered onto the sand and its small black eyes following their movements. Cain wasn't sure if it was relaxing or waiting to strike, but he had seen his brother touch every animal he named. He was determined to name it so he took a deep breath and took a few slow steps closer. The turtle didn't move and finally Cain reached out his finger.

The wet shell was softer than the turtles in the river behind their house.

"It's soft." Cain said surprised.

"Soft-shelled turtle is a great name!" Adam smiled. Cain watched his dad write *soft-shelled turtle* beside the turtle drawing.

"*Soft-shelled turtle.*" Cain whispered to himself with pride.

After the turtle slumped back into the water, Cain beamed with pride, nearly bursting with excitement as they continued walking along the bank of the river.

Abel, determined to outshine his older brother, climbed down from his father's shoulders and pulled out his small bow. He spent the rest of the day scanning the bushes for creatures, a short wooden arrow at the ready.

Adam sat in the sand engrossed in his scrolls, drawing and re-drawing the branch snake and soft-shelled turtle. Cain watched his younger brother miss two foxes, six rats, and four rabbits.

So Cain sat in the warm sand and waited. But as the afternoon wore on, Cain started to worry about his mom. He had never left her and baby Seth home alone this long. He skipped stones in the current to distract himself, but a long list of chores kept stacking up in his mind. He needed to milk the cows, pick the berries, get fresh water, change Seth's soiled clothes . . . and as the sun disappeared behind the trees Cain couldn't wait any longer.

"Do you want some help?" Cain asked, knowing he was a much better shot.

"No. *I'm* gonna bring home dinner." Abel yelled as he searched for an arrow lost in a bush.

"Dad, we should probably get going," Cain said, throwing the rest of his smooth stones into the river.

"Not until I get something!"

"Let's let your brother catch something first," Adam said, not looking up from his scroll.

The clouds overhead were a deep reddish purple by the time one of Abel's arrows stuck in the neck of a baby rabbit.

Cain sighed with relief. He nudged his father, who was still drawing.

"Let's go," Cain pleaded. As they climbed the hill it was Cain who was leading the way. His robe was wet again but now the water felt cold against his skin. The forest bustled with new sounds, hoots and croaks. His stomach rumbled with hunger and he worried that there were other hungry mouths with sharp teeth and big claws out there, watching them. Cain cluched his stomach and pulled his father's hand forward.

But Adam couldn't be rushed. Stopping to sketch flowers and mushrooms he saw dotting the trail, even as the last light faded from the sky. Abel up on his shoulders, his tired eyes closing for long stretches. In the shadowy trails they got turned around, and after they passed what Cain was sure was the same fork in the path, the trail opened into a large clearing.

At the center of the clearing was a tall tree, twice as tall as those around it. Its main branches were as thick as Cain's body and covered with long stringy branches that hung down like snarled hair. Each branch ended with a beautiful red and orange fruit with an almost skin-like rind. The clearing was filled with long thick roots that climbed under and over each other in every direction. There were no shrubs, and the dirt was cold and dry. The tree must have drunk all the water, Cain thought.

Adam whistled, "That is a *beautiful* tree."

"Let's bring some of the fruit home!" Abel said, his short arms grasping for a fruit hanging just out of his reach.

"It looks delicious." Adam grabbed a fruit with both hands and gently tugged it from the branch.

"I bet it's a healing fruit!" Abel smiled.

"It sure smells delicious." Adam breathed in deeply. "Cain open your bag, buddy."

Cain held his small leather satchel open as his father gently placed three of the fruits, each the size of his head, inside his now bulging bag. Cain winced as the satchel's leather strap dug into his shoulder.

"You gonna be able to carry it?" Adam smiled, steadying Cain's shoulder.

"I can carry it." Cain leaned hard to keep his body from tipping over.

"I want to carry one!" Abel shouted.

"You carry your rabbit. That's enough for you," Adam replied.

Cain shot a smug smile up at his brother who was perched on top of their dad's shoulders. "Put me down! I want to walk." Abel insisted, his small hand punching Adam's shoulder.

The three walked through the dark in a tired silence. Cain switched the heavy satchel from shoulder to shoulder every few paces.

When they finally left the forest, the sky was purple and dotted with red clouds. Cain could hear the cows calling from home. He felt his chest tighten and the day's excitement was replaced with worry over all the things he had left undone. The vegetables needed watering, cows and goats needed milking, the eggs gathered, the tall grass around the house still needed to be burned, firewood chopped, the berries needed picking . . . and the list went on. Cain pulled the satchel up against his back and hurried along the winding dirt path home, leaving Adam and Abel behind him.

Once he was through the wooden gate, he hurried to the stable and milked the first cow he saw. Then using the weight of the satchel to counterbalance the nearly full jar of milk, Cain made his way along the small path though the tall dry grass into their darkened house.

Cain could hear his mother and baby brother Seth gently snoring in a duet from her bedroom nearby. He quietly struck the flints together a few times to light the oil lamps on the dining room table.

"Cain?" Eve called with a gravelly voice. "Cain, is that you?" She had clearly been sleeping.

"Don't worry, mom, it's just me," he whispered, peeking his head into her dark bedroom. Her back was propped against the wall and her legs were hidden under blankets. She was exactly where Cain had left her. The only change in the room was that the water, berries, and bread he had left her that morning had been eaten. He dropped the satchel on the dirt floor and one of the fruits rolled out toward the bed.

"We missed you," she whispered.

"I missed you too." Cain smiled and kissed her on the cheek before he lit the bedside lamp. The warm glow illuminated Eve's tired eyes and sallow cheeks. He picked Seth up off the bed and gently lay his sleeping brother on the floor.

"Hey, buddy," Cain whispered in a light, bubbly voice, gently tickling Seth's belly. Seth woke up and his wide brown eyes rolled around the room before resting on Cain. He tossed Seth's wet clothes into a basket, wiped and rewrapped Seth in fresh cloth, before laying him back down on the bed. Eve rubbed Cain's earlobe appreciatively. A spark of joy ran from his ear all the way down to his toes.

"How was your day?" Eve asked. He poured her a small cup of milk. He thought about telling her that they had found a branch snake. That he was so scared when the turtle popped his head out. But then dad had let him name it. But then he thought about her lying in bed all day, and all the chores he had skipped, and Cain swallowed his excitement.

"The walk was kinda boring."

Eve's eyes flashed with a brief smile. "I definitely don't miss hiking."

They sat on the bed in silence until Seth started to gently snore.

Cain remembered going on long walks in the woods with his mom and dad. Riding up on Adam's shoulders, and Abel wrapped tight against his mom's chest. He remembered her strong hands digging out bright pink and yellow flowers to replant them along the fence in their garden. His dad would stuff his pockets with tree nuts and berries, and fill scroll after scroll with drawings of the strange animals they found.

But something had changed when Seth was born. The night of the birth Cain sat at the dinner table just outside his mom's bedroom. His stomach knotted as he listened to her scream in pain. His dad sat next to him nervously eating berry after berry from a wooden bowl. All night he watched the midwife run out of the room with blood-stained sheets, then return with her arms full of water and fresh bedding.

"Was it like this when I was born?" Cain had asked during a long terrible silence.

"It's always like this." Adam winced as his wife screamed again. Cain didn't remember falling asleep. But when he woke up, his head was on the table. He could see his mother was lying still on the bed. His new baby brother, Seth, lay next to her. Her head was in the sunlight. She wasn't moving. She looked dead. He walked to her bed and gently nudged her. She made a guttural sound and he felt his stomach unclench.

But when Eve finally woke up, she was different. It was hard for Cain to say how exactly. She didn't pay attention to what was happening. She kept forgetting things, and she barely ate. Day after day she lay in bed, her legs under the covers, Seth beside her. The brightness in her eyes slowly faded into a dull tiredness. Her body was still there, but part of her was gone.

After month's her rosy, plump cheeks became pale and hollow. Her treasured flower garden grew wild and filled with dead branches and weeds. Rabbits and deer began to eat the vegetables. The grass grew long and wild. Eve finally struggled to produce milk and Adam started feeding Seth cow's milk in the mornings before she woke up and late at night after Eve had fallen asleep.

During the day Adam would take Abel on long hikes, just the two of them. They'd leave early in the morning before Cain woke up. On the first of these walks Cain found a note his dad had left for Eve. Adam wrote that he had left to work on his scrolls and that she was now responsible for taking care of the house and the garden. Cain looked at his mother asleep on her bed. He put the note in his pocket and walked to the garden. He milked the cows and goats, and then swept the house. He placed a bowl of berries and a cup of milk by his mother's bed and one on the table from his father and Abel. When Adam returned he smiled and nodded at Cain who felt tired, but proud of his work.

The next day the muscles in Cain's arms and legs ached. But he forced his tired body out of bed. To make the walk around the garden more manageable Cain decided to use a flaming log to clear a path through the tall grass. Slowly lighting the stalks then stamping them out with his sandal.

Each day his chores felt a little more manageable, until the snake came. Cain had caught glimpses of something in the garden. Flashes of brown and yellow, the end of a tail disappearing around a corner. He began carrying his bow and arrow everytime he left the house.

He was picking berries when he heard his mom scream. He ran back to the house with the bow out and an arrow notched. He found his mom sobbing, the bed covered in blood. The snake had come into the house and bit her on the heel as she slept.

"What if it had bit Seth!" Adam shouted at her that night. She should have never let the grass get so long, he said. It was her fault that she'd been bit. She couldn't just lie in bed. There was work to do. Their sons needed a mother.

Cain sat the dinner table watching. He had never seen his father yell at her before. Adam's fist balled up as if he was going to hit her. And his mom just lay in bed, silently staring at the wall. Tears rolled down her pale cheeks and onto her pillow. He felt a knot in his chest. This was all his fault. He should have burned *all* the grass. He should have told someone that there was a snake in the yard.

"It's my fault." Cain said quietly.

"What?" Adam shouted at him.

"I should have burned all the grass," Cain said, trying to hold back tears of his own.

Adam stared at his son and balled up his fist. "Don't let it happen again."

Cain nodded. Then he walked past his father and picked up Seth, who was crying in his soaking wet clothes. Cain laid Seth down on floor and changed him. After Adam left the room, Cain smiled at his mom. She gave a faint smile back and reached out to rub Cain's earlobe. Cain felt a shiver of warmth run through his body. Cain spent the next three weeks in the garden with a bow and arrow slung over his shoulder, burning the grass, and stamping the flames out.

Cain sat on the side of the bed in silence next to his mother, his legs dangling just above the dirt floor. The smell of smoke and cooked rabbit blew in through the window.

"Abel spent the whole afternoon shooting at rabbits," Cain said, watching his dad scrape the back of the rabbit's fur as Abel fed small sticks into the growing fire.

"You think they're going to share any meat with us?" Eve smiled from the corner of her mouth.

"It kinda looked like a *baby* rabbit," Cain shrugged.

Eve smirked. "Did *you* bring something back for me?" pointing at the red and orange fruit lying on the dirt floor by the satchel.

Cain had forgotten about the fruit. He slid off the bed and picked it up. "It's a new fruit we found," Cain smiled, handing it to her. "Dad thinks it's a healing fruit," he added. Eve turned it over in her hands, rubbing the dimpled skin.

"Should we try it?" She flashed a smile.

"If you want to." Over the years, they had tried feeding her every type of healing leaf, flower, petal, mushroom, fruit, and milk in the forest. But nothing had helped.

She sat up higher in the bed as she pulled the red and orange skin apart. Inside were clusters of bright green seeds. She took one seed and placed it on her tongue.

"It's sweet," she said, then her lips puckered and she coughed. "And tart." She ate them one by one and then rolled the final green seed around in the palm of her hand before chewing it. Cain lay on her chest, hugging her tightly. She rubbed his earlobe.

"Hopefully I'll feel better in the morning." She said, kissing his head.

"I shot this rabbit for you, mommy!" Abel ran into the room holding a tipping plate of thin slices of meat. Abel crawled onto the bed and elbowed Cain out of the way. Spilling red meat grease on the blanket. He held the tipping plate right up to their mother's face. She opened her eyes wide and smiled as she picked up a stringy brown piece off the plate. For years Cain had watched her force herself to look excited whenever Abel and Adam were around.

"Oh, it's hot," she whispered, blowing on it before putting it into her mouth. "But it *is* delicious," she said, scruffing Abel's hair.

Cain reached for a piece of meat but his brother pulled the plate away. "It's *all* for mommy!" Abel shouted.

"Shhhh." Cain punched Abel's shoulder and whispered, "Seth is sleeping. You're gonna wake him up."

"Ow." Abel said. He took an exaggerated bite of meat, clearly taunting Cain.

"Give me some!" Cain said, unable to hold his voice down.

"Shhh." Abel smiled deviously, as Cain fell right into his trap.

Cain clenched his fist. He wanted to punch Abel right in his stupid smiling face.

Eve put her hands on her son's shoulders and whispered, "Abel, thank you for the rabbit but . . ." Eve pointed to the sleeping baby beside her. Abel smiled at his mom, then shot a mean look at Cain before jumping down from the bed and leaving the room. Cain sat in the now quiet room, looking at the final piece of rabbit meat resting on her lap.

"Have some," she pushed it toward Cain. He bit into the warm tender meat, the delicious juices filling his mouth.

"Now let mommy get some sleep. And hopefully I'll feel all better in the morning," she said, rubbing his earlobe. Cain hugged her around her neck and carefully rolled off the bed, blew out the oil lamp, and left the room.

Cain lay under his blankets for a long time in the dark, trying not to think about all the fun things he would do if his mom got out of bed in the morning.

Cain woke suddenly in the dark to the sound of a long painful moan. He lay under the blanket in the dark, hoping he had dreamed it. Then he heard the unmistakeable sound of his mom throwing up on the other side of the wall. He felt a sickening twist in his gut.

Dad said it was a healing fruit. Dad said it was a healing fruit. Dad said it was a healing fruit. He repeated trying to imagine those words coming out of his dad's mouth. But the more he tried to convince himself the less sure he felt. He put his head under his blanket and pretended to be asleep.

Then he heard his father shout, "Cain!" He knew that voice. He remembered his father's anger after the snake bit Eve. *Don't let it happen again*, his dad had said, his fists balled up.

Cain threw back the blankets, crawled across the floor, and climbed out the window into the darkness. His shoulder landed hard on a rock. And for a moment he lay in the long dry grass, his arm throbbing. Then he heard his mother shout in pain and retch again. Cain forced himself to roll over and crawl. He crawled over sharp weeds that stung his hands and rocks that scraped his bare feet.

"Abel! Go find your brother!" Adam's voice cut through the dark.

"Cain!" his brother shouted. Cain crawled to the far end of the garden and then took to the path and finally hid himself under the berry bush. He lay in the dark, quietly gulping air. Again, he heard his mom shout in pain and his mind flooded with memories of the night Seth was born. The midwife running back and forth with water and bloody sheets. Cain pulled his knees to his chest and held his breath.

"Cain! Where are you?" Abel yelled, his voice coming closer. "Dad needs to talk to you *right now!*" Then he saw Abel's small muddy feet through the bushes. "I know you are in there, Cain. So just come out *now!*"

"Why?" Cain said through stifled tears.

Abel got down on his hands and knees, his eyes level with Cain's. "Because you made mom sick!" Abel insisted.

"Dad said it was a healing fruit," Cain said weakly.

"You're supposed to feed fruit to the goats *first,* you idiot!" Abel scoffed as he poked a wooden arrow into the bush. The sharpened point dug into Cain's shoulder. He angrily crawled out of the bush and stood up.

"Stop it!" Cain clenched his fist as he glared down at his younger brother.

"You stop it!" Abel said, poking Cain in the chest with the arrow. "You're the one that made mom sick! I *told* dad not to take you! You mess everything up!" Abel shouted, whipping Cain in the arm.

Cain felt anger boiling up inside him. *Abel had told their dad not to invite him.* How many times had Cain been left at home because of Abel. Abel was big enough to milk cows and pick berries. Abel was old enough to change Seth's dirty clothes. Abel could be helping. He *should* be helping.

Then Cain heard their mom throw up and his anger was split with fear.

"Maybe . . . maybe . . . maybe it was *your* rabbit meat!" Cain said digging his finger hard into Abel's chest.

He heard his father's voice shout, "Cain, *get in here!*"

"Everyone ate the rabbit!" Abel shouted, swinging the arrow at Cain's shoulder. But Cain was ready for it and he blocked the arrow with his forearm. Then he punched Abel right in the face. Hard. Harder than he meant to. Abel's head jerked back and he fell into the grass.

Cain looked down at his brother. In the glow of the yellow moon, he saw Abel lying silent and crooked at his feet, his hair matted with blood. Abel's head had hit a rock hidden in the grass.

Cain shook his brother's limp shoulders. "Abel. Abel," he whispered frantically. Cain tried to wipe the blood off his pale face. "Abel, please wake up, wake up, wake up." Cain sat down and lifted his brother's head onto his lap.

"Help," he said, barely above a whisper. He took a few deep breaths and then shouted, "Dad, *help!*" Cain's shout woke up the night. The cows started mooing and wild dogs in the distance began frantically barking.

Abel opened his eyes. Then Abel touched his face and saw his small fingers covered in blood. He shrieked. "Dad!"

"It's gonna be okay," Cain said, crying tears of relief. "It's gonna be okay." Suddenly Abel's body was illuminated with warm light. Their father stood over the two boys holding a blazing torch. Cain looked up at his father's serious face.

"What happened?" Adam demanded.

Cain looked down at his brother who was screaming and crying. "I . . . I . . ." Adam crouched down and rubbed blood away from Abel's eyes.

"What happened, Abel," Adam asked again, this time his voice softer.

"A snake!" Cain said before Abel could answer. The lie came tumbling out of his mouth. "Abel came to find me. And . . . and a snake . . . a huge snake snapped at Abel and he fell and . . . and . . . and then he hit his head."

Adam stood up and swung the torch around. "Take your brother inside."

Cain helped his sobbing brother to his feet, unable to look up at his father.

"And after you wrap his head, go get more water for your mother. She is having a terrible time passing that fruit you gave her," Adam said with a cold anger.

Cain nodded and walked him back into the house. Out of the corner of his eye he could see his father swing the torch through the long brown grass.

Inside he lifted Abel up onto a chair. His brother's legs kicked wildly as he wrapped Abel's bleeding head in long strips of cloth.

Cain winced as he heard his mother moaning in pain from her bedroom.

When he finished wrapping the bandages, Cain put his hands on his crying brother's shoulders. "All done."

Abel felt the bandages on the back of his head and checked his fingers for blood. When he was sure he had stopped bleeding, Abel sniffed back his tears and hugged Cain.

Cain felt Abel's small arms wrapped tightly around his chest. It had been a long time since Abel hugged him. He forced a smile. "Go lie down, and I'll check on you in a little bit."

"What happened to your brother?" his mom called.

He took a deep breath and walked into her mom's bedroom. The air was thick with the smell of sweat and vomit.

"A snake tried to bite him, and he fell and hit his head," Cain said, looking down at a bowl of green vomit on the floor beside her bed. The last remains of the fruit were now reduced to a disgusting pulp.

"Is he gonna be okay?" she asked. Her head was pale and sweating. The blanket flecked with green bile.

"I wrapped his head," Cain said, climbing on the bed. He felt her sweaty fingers rub his earlobe. His body relaxed. He lay beside her watching through the window as the fire blazed in the grass. He saw illuminated shapes bucking and braying. The cows and goat tied up along the fence. Then he heard her stomach give a long painful-sounding growl.

"I'm sorry I made you sick," Cain said as the tears rolled down his cheeks and onto the blanket.

"Don't worry," she sighed. "It was probably the rabbit meat." The smoke began to blow in through the window and stung Cain's eyes.

"Your father should have never let the grass get so long," Eve whispered as she rubbed Cain's earlobe in the dark.

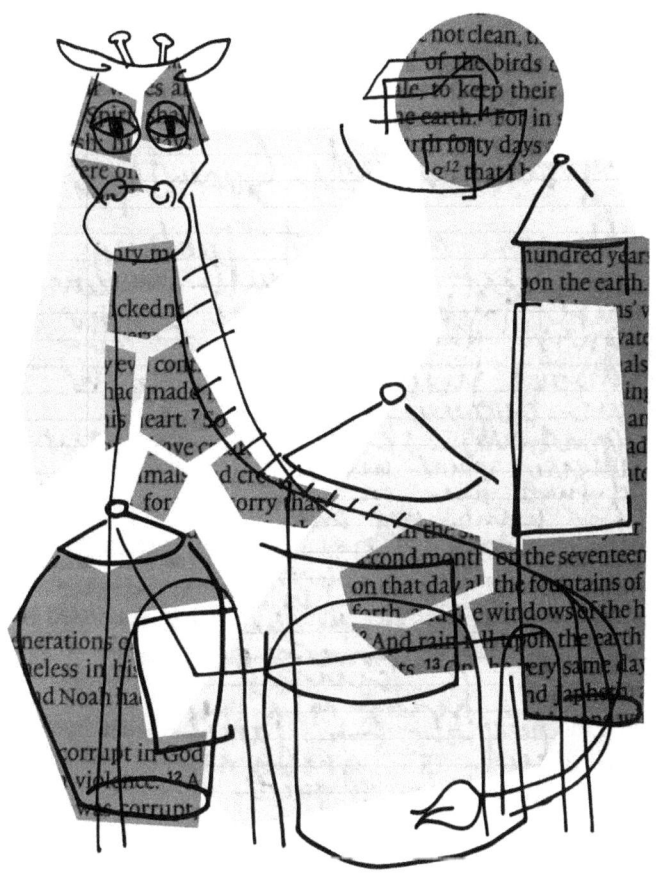

In the days before the flood, people were eating and drinking, marrying and giving in marriage, up to the day Noah entered the ark, they knew nothing about what would happen

—MATTHEW 24:38–39

Naameh and the Ark

Naameh sighed with relief as she entered the cool still air of her shop. She brushed the sand off her robe and unwrapped her long gray hair.

"I was up late stitching," Naameh said as she began to sweep in the dark room. The bones in her knees chirped and her wooden foot banged against floorboards.

"We went back through the guest list I and realized we were going to need more tablecloths." It was five days until the wedding of her youngest daughter, Mal and Naameh had been spending her days in the shop, and her evenings preparing for the wedding—cleaning the ark, sewing new tablecloths and curtains, and finishing the matching wedding robes for her five grandchildren.

Naamah checked the tall jars that lined the walls of her shop. The first jar was full of creamy giraffe's milk. She lifted the second lid—it was empty.

"Only one jar?" Naamah tsked. "Noah wanted to finish the lattice on the fourth floor before the guests arrived."

"Why is there only one jar of giraffe's milk?" Naameh asked again. When no one answered. Namaah finally looked up. She was alone in the shop.

"Old lady talking to herself." She shook her head, quietly laughing at herself, the wrinkles in her plump cheeks gathering around her eyes.

"Mal!" She knocked hard on the door that led to the cellar.

"Hold on a moment," Mal said, running up the stairs with a basket of ostrich eggs hanging from each forearm.

"I was just saying thank you for getting the milk in." Naameh smiled, gently brushing the sand off her daughter's forehead.

"I should have started with the giraffes." Mal explained, a little winded. "By the time I got the first jar the sand was blowing in every direction. I know dad wanted to finish the fourth floor."

"You leave your father to me," Naameh reassured her. "Now, go put those eggs down so we can open the shop. People are already lining up."

Naameh walked to the front door and openned it a crack. A hot gust of sandy air blew in with the first customer.

"Rayah! How are you?" Naameh smiled holding her hands out expectantly. Rayah brushed the dust off as best she could before hugging Naameh.

"Well look at you, you're just covered in sweat and sand." Naamah tsked. Rayah and her daughter made the walk once a week from their small farm just down the road. Always with fresh-cut timber and a dozen eggs. "I wasn't going to come in this wind, but Chalah was sick and I . . ."

"Hold that thought, deary," Naameh cut her off. "It's just too much to ask people to wait out there."

Rayah furrowed her brow. "There's *a lot* of people in line."

"All the more reason. Just tell them to brush off as best they can before they get inside."

"Grab that broom against the wall, Mal." Naameh pointed.

After a lot of bustling, brushing, and shuffling the shop was filled with women of every age in a long line snaking along the walls of the now very hot and very sandy shop.

"Everyone okay?" Naameh looked around smiling reassuringly. There was a cheerful murmur of agreement.

Naameh focused on her first customer, "Now Rayah, you were saying your husband was not feeling well?"

"It's his gut. He saved a flank of ibex that I *told* him to throw away." Rayah looked around at the women, who knowingly nodded to each other. Naameh was tickled. She lived for these stories.

"So I catch him in the middle of the night, mid-flank" Rayah mimicked her husband chewing dead-eyed. "And mind you the meat has already turned green at this point." Rayah's ten-year-old daughter pipes in, "And two hours later he's—" her small body doubled over as she mimicked throwing up. The shop erupted in a chorus of laughter.

"So we need a cup of Noah's giraffe milk in exchange for the wood." Rayah placed the arm's-length timber on the floor. "And one ostrich egg for these," her daughter added, handing Mal the basket of chicken eggs.

Mal ladeled a cup of giraffe's milk and handed them an ostrich egg. "And give them a little extra giraffe's milk. We want Chalah feeling better by your wedding day. Noah is roasting an ostrich and a *fresh* ibex!" Namaah laughed. Mal blushed and the women laughed in anticipation of the big party.

Over the four generations that Noah's family had milked giraffes, it had come to be known as *the* cure-all in the valley. Anyone complaining about gut pain, headaches, sore feet, or a baby two weeks late—giraffe's milk was the cure. It was the first suggestion out of everyone's mouth. And Naameh's shop was the only place to get it.

Naameh never confirmed that giraffe milk had healing properties. But she never denied it. Smiling out of the corner of her plump mouth and touching her nose, she said, "The results speak for themselves."

Noah never interfered in Naameh's shop. And she never commented on how big he built the ark. His one demand was that she only trade giraffe's milk for timbers. "We can't build the ark with egg shells," Noah would repeat whenever the topic came up.

It was late in the afternoon by the time the last woman had left the shop. Mal sat exhausted on the large stack of wood planks.

"Just leave those for the boys to pick up in the morning," Naameh said, wiping the sweat from her forehead. "I don't imagine they got much work done in this wind."

Outside the shop, the wind whipped back and forth under the gray clouds that covered the valley like a blanket. Naameh leaned on Mal's arm as they slowly navigated the sandy path in the long shadow of the massive four-story ark that towered over the two-room mud and stick homes that dotted the now treeless valley. The ark was by far the largest structure in the valley. After visitors got over the initial shock of seeing a four-story boat in the middle of the desert, they would often comment on the smooth timbers that lined the boat's massive hull. The first two floors of the boat were made of long smooth timbers, the last testament to the tall gopher wood trees that had once dotted the valley. But as the eye moved up the ark, the timbers became shorter and shorter, until the fourth floor was nothing more than a patchwork of arm-length wood of different shapes and colors.

They continued along the path. They walking past a pair of giraffes who were eating the last cluster of dusty green leaves off the top of a bush. The ostriches, sittting low over their few remaining eggs, squawked at them as they passed. They continued past the pig pen, past the cows and camels. A particularily cold gust of wind blew across Naameh's cheeks and Mal stopped to stare at a patch of particularly dark clouds.

"The wind will push them right over us," Naamah said, patting her daughter's arm.

"It was never this cold when I was young," Mal grimaced as she tucked her scarf tight.

"People only remember the nice weather," Naameh assured her. "And it's always colder in the shade." Mal knew it was useless to argue so she let it go.

Whether it was age or the weather, Naameh couldn't deny that her knees hurt a little more each time she made her way up the sixteen wooden steps to the small front door of the ark.

Naameh sighed as they stepped into the cool darkness of the ark. The windows in the large main room were all latched shut. She could hear Noah and her sons' hammers pounding upstairs. She stood by the door and shoook the sand off her dress as her eyes adjusted. After a moment she saw the newly polished tables and stools Noah had finished making for the wedding. The craftsmanship was impeccable, each piece perfectly sanded, trimmed, and fitted.

The red curtains hung, nearly touching the floor. She had made them special for Mal's wedding. Naameh ran her hands along the matching red tablecloths, which bore a bright yellow stripe down the middle. They tableclothes were still clean, despite the sand and whatever Noah was working on upstairs. She sighed, looking at the bare tables. She had five days to make three more tablecloths.

Mal sensed her anxiety. "Don't worry, we have plenty of help to finish everything."

They walked past the hand-carved signs on the small side rooms. They read: ibex, llama, zebra, cow. Naameh had reorganized each room to hold all the extra curtains, tablecloths, plates, cups, and candles she had collected from all the weddings, funerals, and holidays.

Naameh slowly made her way up the first set of stairs, the tap of her wooden foot lost in the hammering upstairs. A wave of frustration hit her as she opened the door to the storeroom and saw dozens of massive sacks of beans, rice, and hay scattered across the floor. Noah, Shem, Ham, and Japheth were nailing together a row of shelves.

Noah stopped. He looked at Naameh and then down at the mess on the floor as if seeing it for the first time, his hammer hanging guiltily by his side. "We finished the last set of tables and chairs. And then I saw those clouds roll in and I wanted to re-check the supply deck in case it rai—"

Naameh raised her eyebrow and Noah stopped. Mal came up the stairs and pointed at the shelves incredulously. "Are these shelves for the wedding?"

Noah forced a toothy smile. "There was a whole mess of chickens roosting in the bean stores. So we started cleaning them out and decided we needed more shelving."

Naameh took a deep breath. "Well, just finish it up. We already have plenty to do."

"How much wood did you get today?" Noah asked pointing at his dwindling stack of timbers. "I suppose people stayed home on account of the wind."

"No one showed up." Naameh lied casually, hoping to get a rise out of him. "And Rayah told me Chalah was sick, so I sent her home with the rest of the giraffe's milk."

"You didn't!" Noah looked at her aghast. "There was a weeks worth of milk in that jar! We were gonna put up—"

"I'm just getting you, you old grouch," Naameh laughed. "Everyone huddled into the shop."

"And you . . ."

"And I made sure to get your wood." Naameh rolled her eyes and started up the stairs.

"You'd give the roof away if it wasn't nailed down," Noah muttered to himself.

"What was that?" Naameh stopped on the stairs.

"It's a business, is all I'm saying," Noah said louder.

"We have a wedding in five days is all *I'm* saying." She pointed at the disorganized sacks on the floor.

"We roasted up the chickens," Noah said, eager to change the subject. "I'll make you a plate."

Naameh stopped on the third floor to give hugs and kisses to her five small grandchildren playing on the floor with carved wooden animals. Her knees were sore and her legs burned by the time she made it up the final set of stairs to her bedroom perched on the deck of the ship.

She sat down on her bed. Outside her bedroom window the clouds were still looming, now darker as the sun was setting. The wind didn't seem have moved them. Naameh untied the leather straps to her wooden foot and massaged her stump. The skin was thick and calloused and her calf muscle was tight and sore.

From her bed she could see smoke rising from the cooking fires burning at the homesteads that dotted the valley. She could see the small frames of Rayah and her daughter hunched over a fire outside their one-room clay house.

She remembered being a small girl and sitting around the cooking fire, her mother reassuring her, "You'll find somebody." The other mothers nodded along, "Oh yes . . ." their voices overflowing with so much pity that Naameh was convinced there was absolutely no way she would *ever* find someone to marry her.

Naameh remembered the first time she had seen the ark. She was fourteen and had finally managed to convince her mother that she could navigate the rocky hills that seperated their valley from the ark. Naameh had stood in awe as she watched Noah's father Lamech on a tall ladder. He was hammering long timbers onto the unfinished second story. Noah had handed her a cup of giraffe's milk. She noticed his fingers were stained the color of the timbers.

"Why is your dad building that boat?" she asked.

"A flood," Noah shrugged. "Someday this whole valley is gonna be underwater." His hand panned across the hills surrounding them.

Naameh remembered trying to imagine the ark bobbing up and down on water the way sticks floated in the puddles in her garden.

"When?" she asked nervously. It had never rained enough to even cover her ankle.

Noah shrugged again. "What's wrong with your foot?" he asked, pointing at her calloused stump. Naameh tried to stand up as straight as she could, took a deep breath, and with as much pride as she could muster she said, "I don't have one."

Noah bent down, examining it. He rubbed the few dark hairs sprouting out of his chin. Then picked up a small wooden timber the same color as the ark. He held it next to her stump and used his knife to mark the distance between her stump and the ground. Naameh stood there waiting for him to say something. But Noah had just walked away with the timber.

"What did he want?" Naameh's mother asked, holding Naameh's hand on the walk home.

"Do you think the valley is gonna flood?" Naameh asked.

Her mother squeezed her hand. "Noah's father is a little . . ." she paused looking for a polite word. "He isn't well. In here." She pointed at her forehead.

The next week Naameh and her mother came back to get more giraffe's milk.

"I made this for you," Noah said, handing her a piece of polished wood with tangled leather straps hanging off it. She ran her hands up and down the smooth the dark wood. She didn't have any idea what it was.

"Well, try it on," Noah said wiping his hands on his sawdust-covered apron.

Noah untangled the leather straps and placed the wood in the sand. That's when Naameh realized it was a wooden foot. She felt her heart beat faster. She put her other foot next to it. The wooden foot was nearly the same size. She cautiously rested her stump in the wooden ankle. She felt Noah's fingers against her skin as he wrapped the leather straps around her calf.

She slowly put some weight on the wooden foot. It slipped in the sandy ground but she quickly regained her balance. The watching mothers nodded in approval.

Naameh's mother smiled at her daughter and then walked over to talk to Lamech, who was up on a ladder hammering a timber. Lamech seemed quite oblivious to what was going on. Naameh watched her mother talk politely up at him. He stopped hammering and nodded along to her mother's words. The next day Naameh was told that she and Noah were arranged to be married.

Naameh sat on the edge of the bed massaging her stump. The last gray light of the evening was fading. There was a knock at the bedroom door. Mal came in holding a plate of roasted chicken and a cup of giraffe's milk.

"They finished the shelves," Mal sighed, sitting down next to Naameh on the bed.

"How do they look?" Naameh asked taking a bite of warm, greasy chicken.

"Good."

Naameh didn't know why she had asked. Everything Noah made, down to the wooden nails, was beautiful.

"Get some sleep, we have *a lot* of sewing tomorrow," Naameh said, patting Mal's knee.

After Mal had left, Naameh sipped the giraffe's milk and watched the dark clouds shift in place. Then she saw a drop of water land on the windowsill. Her heart jumped into her throat. She put down the milk and quickly wiped the raindrop away. Her heart beating fast, she stuck her hand out of the window, her palm open. She felt sand blowing on her fingers, but no rain. "Please don't let it rain until after the wedding," she whispered to herself.

Noah came into the bedroom long after dark. Naameh was putting the final stitches into her granddaughter's red and yellow robe. A candle burned on the bedside table. She glanced at the window; the sill was dry. Noah sat down on the edge of the bed and stared out the window.

"Clouds are getting darker," he said.

"The wind will push them right over us," Naameh reassured him, not looking up from her stitching. "Get some sleep, we have a lot to do for tomorrow's dinner." Naameh put her sewing needles down and blew out the candle. But long after Noah had begun to snore, Naameh lay in bed watching the windowsill.

At dinner the next night, the main room of the ark was filled with the smell of darkly roasted nuts and meats. The new tables were decorated with the bright new red and yellow cloths. Candles dripping onto freshly polished candle sticks, and bowls filled with pomegranates and olives.

Naameh sat next to her husband, their three sons, their wives, and five grandchildren. Mal sat smiling next to her future husband, Arom, his mother and father, and his two younger sisters. His family had arrived that afternoon from the next valley to prepare for the wedding.

"This is much nicer than I had expected," Arom's father said between large bites of meat. "When Arom said you were a boat maker I expected more of a—" Arom kicked his father under the table. Mal's face flushed red. She had told Arom's family not to talk about the boat or rain or the clouds.

"We need a boat big enough for my whole family," Noah smiled with a finger wagging. "With enough food to last at least until the next growing season."

Naameh put her hand on Noah's lap. "This is Mal's night," she whispered in his ear. The rest of the table shifted uncomfortably and focused on their food.

Arom's father continued on, his lips curled into a faint mocking smile. "We had a lot of rain last week." Mal put her food down and glared at her future father-in-law, who carried on. "A few of the homesteads in our valley collapsed and a cow got stuck in the mud. Couldn't get it out. After it stopped raining they got the whole village to come and eat it right there."

"And that was just a light rain. I keep telling people not to build so close to the river," Noah scoffed, quickly eating a handful of olives one at a time. His knee bounced under Naameh's hand.

"How big of a boat do you think we would need if this flood of yours ever happened?" Arom's father smirked. His questions were clearly getting the intended reaction out of Noah. "How many people could we fit in here? Two hundred? A thousand? I bet you have a year's worth of beans and rice up there." He said pointing a meat flecked T-bone up the stairs.

"We?" Noah cleared his throat. "You live much too far away to use this boat in a flood." Noah rubbed his gray beard. "But I would be happy to send you home with enough wood to get started on your own boat. It would be pretty small but you could try and paddle to the ark. Of course we would have to get more stores," Noah started thinking out loud.

Arom's father smirked as Noah prattled on. The rest of the table watched in uncomfortable silence.

Naameh patted Noah's knee. "*If* it floods, we can make room—"

"—Naameh," Noah muttered, cutting her off.

Naameh raised her voice above her husband, "But the animals are coming with us, and if you get shit on you . . ." She sneered at Arom's father. "I don't want to hear a *word* about it." She stood up to change the subject. "Now I need this table cleared and someone to wash the candlesticks and the tablecloth." She clapped her hands for people to get to work.

That night Noah paced back and forth next to their bed. "Why did you tell them they could use the ark? My father always said 'If the valley floods, it will flood hard and fast.' That cow got stuck in the mud after a night of light rain."

Naameh sighed, stitching her last tablecloth, "How many people came to your boat-building class?"

A few years back there had been a hard rain and a child had drowned in the mudslide. Afterward, Noah had been able to convince a few of the villagers to build their own boats. But after months without rain, Noah was left with three half-built row boats and no students.

Noah sat down on the end of the bed, his knee bouncing. "Those are heavy rain clouds," he said, watching the dark clouds outside his window.

"Just try and get some sleep," Naameh said as she put her away her nearly completed tablecloth and blew out the bedside candle.

Naameh woke in the dark to the sound of rain tapping on the wood. The windowsill was covered in water. Noah was still sleeping next to her, his guttural snores booming over the rain. She was still, desperately hoping the storm didn't wake him up. She tried to ever so slowly pull the blankets up over his head to dampen the sound.

Then a bolt of lightning punctuated the dark with silent light. Naameh's stomach twisted, she waited for a moment hoping against hope that it wouldn't thunder. Then a moment later the night exploded with a booming crack.

Noah sat upright and wide-eyed. He listened to the rain tapping against the roof of the bedroom. "Noah," she said rubbing his back. "Now let's not wake everyone up just yet. It's just a light rain," she said pointing at the sill.

Lighting flashed again. Then another loud, echoing thunder. Noah got out of bed and quickly pulled his robe over his head, his wild gray hair twisted in every direction. "We need to get the animals inside."

"Noah, please, the wedding," Naameh said forcefully. Noah stood next to the bed as if torn. "We have it all set up," Naameh pleaded. "We would have to take out all the wedding tables and put everything else in storage. And then take it all back out—" Lightning struck and boomed. Noah ran his hand along the wet windowsill and shook his head, "Better to be safe."

He ran into the hallway. "Everyone wake up!" His voice echoed down the stairs.

"Noah! We have to at least put away the tablecloths and curtains!" She shouted, now angry. But he was gone.

"Ham, Shem, Japheth! Get Up! GET UP!" She heard Noah shouting. She wanted to chase him down and tackle him. But she knew she would never catch him.

She sat in the bed and watched the window, hoping it would stop raining before Noah got to the front door. "Please stop raining. Please stop raining."

Then she heard the heavy main door to the ark creak open and Noah blew the ram's horn. It blasted loud and flat, echoing through the ark. Then Noah shouted, "Line 'em up!"

Naameh took a frustrated breath and threw back the covers, forcing herself out of the warm bed and into the cold wet night.

She slipped her robe on, wrapped her hair up, and sat on the edge of the bed as she strapped her wooden foot on.

Holding on to the railing she slowly made her way down the first set of stairs in the dark. Her wooden foot banged hard against the steps. She stopped outside the bedrooms. The children were awake, a few were on the beds playing with their wooden animals. Naameh made eye contact with Mal who had tears in her eyes. Naameh motioned for her to stay there. "I'll handle your father." Mal wiped her eyes and nodded.

Naameh seethed with anger as she descended the final set of stairs. She took a deep breath and opened the door to the main room.

In the belly of the ark it was worse than she could have imagined. Her heart fell as she saw a huge muddy ibex with its horns caught in the legs of a chair and swinging it around wildly. "No!" she shouted. In the chaos of mud and animals she could see her new tablecloths being trampled under cow hooves, and a pair of camels had kicked the tables against the wall. Ham was pulling some curtains from the mouth of a ram. Japheth and Shem were standing in front of the closets full of the spare supplies and shouting at Noah.

"Get those animals in their pens!" Noah shouted halfway up the ramp, pulling a pair of donkeys who were bucking and braying.

Outside the first red streaks of morning light showed the rain had slowed to a very fine mist. Smoke was streaming from smoldering fires dotting the homesteads across the valley. "Stop!" she shouted through tears of anger and disappointment. "The rain is stopping!" she pointed outside the ark.

Noah caught her eye and turned to look at the clouds. He was soaked and caked in mud. But he put his hand up and felt the mist. The animals continuing to bray and buck in the wreckage of her daughter's wedding. After a few moments the rain stopped altogether.

Naameh shouted with a cold anger, "Noah, I told you—" but she stopped herself, afraid of what she might say next. Then she took a deep breath. "Get these animals out of here."

Noah held his dirty palm up for a moment. It had stopped raining. He let go of the donkeys and they ran back down the ramp.

Noah sat down and watched the clouds as he rubbed his muddy beard. Her sons whipped the remaining animals outside. As her sons whipped the rest of the animals out of the room, Naameh stood at the top of the stairs. "I told you—"

"I'll clean it up," he cut her off, a mixture of frustration and shame in his voice.

"You will," Naameh's voice quivered with anger. "You will fix these chairs and tables by tomorrow night." Noah nodded, still looking up at the clouds, his hand in the air feeling for rain.

Naameh spent the morning on her hands and knees with her daughters-in-law scrubbing mud, shit, and sand. The salvagable tablecloths and curtains soaked in buckets outside. Naameh told them to take their time, dig out the corners, scrub the knots in the timber. She had forbidden Mal from seeing the wreckage until after it was cleaned.

By late afternoon they were able to pull out a fresh set of fabrics and begin redecorating. Mal came down before dinner to a half-decorated, but very clean room.

"We still have two days to get it all ready. And your father said he could fix all the tables and chairs," Naameh sighed, opening the door to the main room.

Mal gasped in disappointment before forcing a look of gratitude. Naameh looked at the room with fresh eyes and realized how much worse it looked. It was half full of chairs. Two of the six tables were deeply scarred with hooves and horns. The tablecloths and curtains were mismatched. Only one red and yellow tablecloth had survived.

"Thank you for working so hard," Mal nodded optimistically through tears of disappointment she couldn't fight back.

"And remember we still have two days," Naameh said rubbing her back. Mal broke down sobbing.

"It will be just fine. People won't even notice."

"What about Amor's family?" Mal said, wiping her tears.

"We will just have to uninvite them." Naameh chuckled.

That night Noah sat on the end of the bed, his knee bouncing in agitation. He watched dark clouds flash with lightning. Noah winced at each crack of thunder. Naameh lay on the bed facing the wall. "The river is already full," Noah said. "Another rain like last night . . ."

"Stop it, Noah," Naameh said with a cold anger. Noah's bouncing knee was shaking the bed. Naameh missed her stich because of the bouncing and tried to swallow her anger.

"It could be raining up river," he whispered.

"You are not going to ruin this wedding for Mal," she snapped back.

Lightning flashed and immediately cracked with the sound of a tree splitting open. Naameh felt the room get very cold. She pulled up another blanket in silence.

"We spent all day digging mud out of the timbers and you don't have time to fix any more chairs. So let it go," Naameh said.

Noah sat watching the sky in silence. His whole body was shaking. Lighting struck again, and again. Naameh forced herself to keep sewing despite her growing anxiety.

Then out of the corner of her eye she saw small droplets on the windowsill. "Do not go downstairs," Naameh said.

Noah sat still on the bed, staring at the windowsill. A moment later, the skies opened up and released a torrential downpour.

Naameh put down her sewing, her heart clenched, as she watched it rain harder than she had ever seen.

"This is it," Noah said quietly. Naameh could barely hear his words under the sound of rain lashing the wooden roof of their bedroom.

"Don't."

Noah stood up, pleading to his wife. "I'm sorry, but the riverbanks are going to overflow. Then the valley."

"Sit down," Naameh demanded.

"We have to get the animals inside." Noah watched the thick sheets of rain begin to pool on the deck of the ark. "We should at least send word to Arom and his family," Noah said, stroking his gray beard nervously.

"Sit down."

Naameh and Noah watched it rain for a long time. The wall of rain right outside the window was too loud and thick to see or hear anything in the valley. Naameh could barely hear the thunder over the sounds of water hitting the wooden roof.

Naameh was struggling to keep her eyes open when she heard the wood walls of the ark let out a deep groan. Then the ark moved, and Naameh's stomach lurched. It was strange to feel something so huge move. She looked at Noah, unsure for the first time. Noah stood up and ran down the stairs.

"Noah, wait!" she shouted after him. But her words were lost in the rain and groaning wood.

She dressed as quickly as she could, still hoping to stop him. She made her way down the first set of stairs. Then the wood moaned loudly and the ark began to tip sideways. Naameh held onto the railing and waited for a moment. The stairs were now at a steeper incline. She slowly stepped down each step, making sure to keep her wooden foot from slipping.

Naameh passed the bedrooms. Her grandchildren were all huddled on their mother's beds. Mal shouted something Naameh couldn't hear. Naameh motioned for her to stay with the children.

She continued down the stairs, her muscles and joints aching. She stopped outside the door to the main room, emotionally preparing herself for whatever she saw on the other side.

She took a deep breath and pushed opened the door and was hit with a cold rain that soaked her robe. As the lightning flashed Naameh could see the rain pouring horizontally into the ark. Lightning cracked and she saw animals bucking and crying, tables and chairs scattering and breaking underfoot. Rain poured down the wooden ramp into the ark. Noah, Ham and Japheth stood knee deep in foamy water, leaning back as they struggled for footing to pull the crank that closed the massive door.

Lightning reflected again and Naameh covered her mouth in disbelief. Outside the lightning illuminated the valley filled with water. She could see the shadow of two goats standing on the roof of her shop. A donkey was crying as it struggled to swim just out of reach of the ramp, still hanging half open.

"No!" Naameh screamed. "We can't—" Naameh shouted. Then the door closed and the room was dark. The sound of rain was replaced by a cacophony of animals kicking and biting in the water.

She planted her bare foot as best she could on each wet step. She had to tell Noah to stop closing the door. There were still people out there. She stepped into cold water. Her leg was swallowed up to her thigh. She could feel grains of sand swirling around her skin, her wooden foot slipping. Then she felt a hoof kick into her side. She fell to her knees and gasped for breath, the cold sandy water now soaking her up to her chest. She took sharp shallow breaths, watching hooves, water, and wood jut at her from the darkness.

Then Naameh felt a strong hand under her arm, pulling her out of the water. It was her son Shem.

"We can't—" she whispered through painful breaths. But she stopped when the wood groaned deep and long and the ark lurched again. Naameh felt her stomach fall. She leaned on her son, her ribs aching against his body. He slowly guided her back up the stairs. Then Shem shut the door between them.

Naameh stood on the stairs alone. Her clothes heavy and cold. She felt her mind go loose and her breath quicken. Naameh heard shouting, but it felt far away. She willed herself to walk up the first steep step, her cold knee searing with sharp pain.

One step at a time, she pulled herself up by the railing. Finally stopping at the door in front of the door to the storeroom. She opened the door. It was dark inside. The smell of beans, rice, and grains thick in the damp air. The only sound was the rain against the walls of the ark. She couldn't see so she reached out and ran her hands along the new shelves Noah had built. In the dark she could still feel the sawdust on the timbers. She thought of her mother who had promised to bring a bag of rice to the wedding. Naameh had insisted that they had enough, not to bother herself.

Naameh took a few deep tear-filled breaths. She wondered where her mother had slept. If she had already left for the wedding. Then she thought of Rayah and her daughter, and of the two goats on the roof of her shop, the donkey frantically swimming just below the ramp. In the dark, her mind swirled as she pictured neighbor after neighbor who were likely out in the rain and the rising water.

As her eyes adjusted, she walked past the shelves and un-latched a small wooden window. It swung open. Through the gray morning light and sheets of rain she could see water as far as the hills surrounding the valley. Looking down she saw brown water crashing against the side of the ark. The roof of her shop was gone. The animal pens were gone. Rayah and Chalah's house was gone.

She closed the window and tried to think of what do next. Then she felt the leather straps wet and painfully tight against her ankle. In the rush she had tied the leather straps too tight.

She sat down on a sack of rice and untied the straps. The stump skin was numb and cold to the touch. She sat for a long time in the dark and massaged the feeling back into her stump. She took deep breaths as tears rolled down her cheeks. *It's morning. The children will need breakfast. I can make porridge.* The thoughts came one by one. *There is a water in the rain barrels on the top floor.*

The ark heaved and she felt her stomach turn. She finally spoke, "It's morning, and I need to make breakfast for my children and grandchildren." Saying it out loud helped ground her. Her children was still safe in their bedrooms. They had survived.

She carefully retied the leather straps. They felt cold against her skin. She picked up a small sack of rice, and walked toward the door, her wooden foot banging hard against the wooden floor. Then she took a deep breath, wiped her eyes, and stepped out of the storeroom.

"Come, let us build ourselves a city, with a tower that reaches to the sky, so that we may make a name for ourselves; otherwise we will be scattered over the face of the whole earth."

—GENESIS 11:4

The Unplanned City of Babel

Bab-el stood wrapped in a thick wool blanket, as the cold morning wind whipped across the roof of the tower. The exposed roof was littered with shovels, wheelbarrows, and bricks. All of the abandoned building supplies caked white with bird shit. His toes were numb, and if it had been any other morning, he would have gone back inside. But it was his last morning inprisoned in the tower and maybe his last morning on earth. He tried to keep his hands warm on a hot cup of breakfast tea, watching as the gray morning clouds rose over the sun like cotton over a candle.

Bab-el had tied a thick rope just above his waist. The other end was securely attached to his favorite student, Samir. Her dark brown legs dangled freely over the unfinished ledge of the tower. The six-year-old Ethiopian girl held a long worm between her small fingers. The worm blew slowly back and forth in the wind.

Most people would have been too scared to sit on the ledge of an eleven-story tower, especially on a windy morning. But not Samir. She was so fearless he had to tie a rope around her. He had often wondered if Ethiopians were a more courageous people. He had once seen some Ethiopian builders dangling off the side of the tower with buckets of mortar. But it may have been a product of her growing up without parents, no one to fuss over her. Bab-el, having no children of his own, couldn't be sure.

He felt his tea getting cold as he scanned the horizon for the large white wings they had come to expect just after sunrise. Then
. . .

"Samir, look!" he pointed. In the distance was the outline of a stork gliding through the gray.

Samir held the worm out over the ledge. Bab-el felt the rope tighten around his waist.

"Cee-Cooo Ceeeee-Coo," Samir croaked high and loud.

"Samir, it's in the back of the throat. It's *Ce-Co,* not Ceeeeeeee Coooooo, " Bab-el corrected. He leaned back a little, putting one hand on the rope in case Samir got too excited.

"Ce-Co Ce-Co Ce-Co," Bab-el croaked, his tongue clicking.

Samir took a deep breath and shouted "CEE COO CEE COO!" The stork began to smoothly glide in a wide circle around the tower.

"Well done, Samir," Bab-el whispered. Samir held the worm out farther. Bab-el leaned back a little, pulling her body back from the ledge.

They watched as the stork glided over the endless piles of rubble and ash that surrounded the tower. As far as the eye could see the valley was strewn with the blackened remains of houses, sheds, shops, carts, and barns sprawling out from the tower in every direction. A nearly great city that Bab-el had been too busy to plan.

What was left after the fire had become oversized bird houses. Sparrows, vultures, ravens, and storks had picked the remains of the city down to the bone and then roosted in its skeleton. At night even the tower echoed with chirps, croaks, and the shrill cries of bats.

"Ce Co Ce Co Ce Co," Bab-el croaked again as the stork began its second lap around the tower. It turned sharply and beat its long black-tipped wings, finally fluttering to a halt next to Samir. It stood for a moment on the ledge. One foot on a brick and one foot on a hardened glob of mortar.

Ke Ke Ke Ke Ke Ke, the stork croaked. Samir was shaking with excitement as she laid the worm on a brick midway between herself and the stork. The stork looked up at Samir. Then stamped its long naked legs on the brick.

"Ke-Ke-Ke-Ke." Bab-el clicked his tongue. It froze with one eye toward him. Bab-el held his breath. Then the stork lowered its pale pink beak and gobbled up the worm.

"Thee-Thee-Thee-Thee?" Samir tried to click her tongue, but what came out sounded more like wheeze. The stork looked at her and then flew away.

"Oooooo," Samir balled her fists and shrieked with joy. "Do you think she understood us?!"

"Maybe. She came and ate," Bab-el smiled. "But it's hard to pick up a language a few clicks and croaks at a time. You just keep taking your notes and we will see if any patterns start to emerge."

Samir unrolled her scroll on the bricks. The edge of the scroll fluttered in the wind. Bab-el watched over her shoulder as she wrote down each of the croaks they had done. His heart swelled with the rare pride of a teacher who sees the best of themselves in a student.

He was really going to miss her.

Their morning bird calling had started as a bribe. The other students in his language class were plodding along at a relatively consistent pace. But Samir was just . . . better. Conjugations, sentence structure, sounds, comparing letters—it was all second nature to her. Her hand shot up to answer before Bab-el had even finished the question. When he finally stopped calling on her she grew bored and began running around the classroom pointing out other children's mistakes.

After a few classes of this, one student got fed up and punched Samir. Bab-el watched Samir sit on the ground rubbing her arm.

She probably deserves it, he had thought to himself. It had taken him a long time to adjust to his own gifts for languages. He had been about her age when his ability had shown itself. As a child it had surprised him to learn that not everyone could speak every language. But when asked how he could, he didn't really know what to say. He would shrug, "I just have an ear for it. Like how a musician can just sing the harmony."

As Samir sat crying on the floor the other students went back to their Egyptian vocabulary words. Bab-el walked over to her and asked. "Samir, would you like to be my *assistant language teacher.*"

"Sounds like a lot of work," she said, sniffing back tears. "What do I get for it?"

Bab-el stifled a smile. A parentless child in the basement of a bat-infested, abandoned tower, and she still had the courage to barter with her teacher. Bab-el stroked his long gray beard and forced his face to look like they were in the midst of a serious business meeting.

"Well you already have room and board in the tower for free so . . ."

"I want to talk to storks." Samir cut him off. Bab-el's bushy eyebrows furrowed in confusion.

Samir looked around a little embarrassed by her request. The other students were all staring at her. She stood up and tried to regain her composure. "Well, that is, if you can actually speak stork," Samir said loud and condescendingly.

Bab-el paused. *Could he learn to speak stork,* he wondered. "I've never tried," he shrugged. "But I'll tell you what. If you help the other kids with their vocab words, you can meet me tomorrow morning on the top floor before class." Samir smiled. "Bring a scroll and a quill . . . and a bowl of worms," he added.

Samir spent the rest of the day bouncing from desk to desk helping the other students. It turned out to be a very productive class.

The next morning Bab-el woke up to the sound of Samir's small sandals clopping up the long spiral staircase. And much to his surprise, it was a welcome change. It had been a long three years living by himself on the top floor. Waking up to the shrill cries of the bats coming up through the floor.

"Kee-Coo Kee-Coo," Samir yelled as the stork flew away. "Ok, now let's spit!" Samir laughed and clicked her heels together with glee. Bab-el had initially regretted letting Samir join him in his morning spit. But as he had yet to hit the guard, he figured it was just a little harmless fun.

Bab-el hacked up some snot and aimed at the tower guard standing at the front door to the tower, eleven stories below. The burly soldier was reduced to the size of an ant with a blade of grass for a spear. Bab-el waited for the wind to stop and spit. Samir watched as his snot wound its way down the brick wall. But near the fourth floor the snot caught a gust of wind and disappeared.

"Too bad," Samir shrugged, then she hacked and spit. Her bubbly snot disintegrated a few floors below. Then Bab-el saw the Cushite Chief, Nimrod, a thick hunter with a necklace of lion's teeth, emerge from one of the few standing houses near the base of the tower. The sight of Chief Nimrod choked out the little bit of hope that Bab-el had nurtured over the last three years. Bab-el had let himself believe that maybe Chief Nimrod would never come back, that maybe Bab-el could convince the other elders to just let him go.

Samir, unaware of Bab-el's fear, cheerfully waved down at Chief Nimrod. "I can't wait to see the look on Chief Nimrod's face when he realizes that I'm smarter than he is," she said gleefully. Chief Nimrod waved back up at her.

"No one like a show off," Bab-el reminded her as he lifted her down from the ledge and untied the rope from her waist. "Now go get our scrolls ready for class." Samir ran across the bird-shit –covered rooftop and disappeared down the spiral stairs, her sandals clopping against the brick.

Bab-el hadn't seen Chief Nimrod since the morning after fire. The entire city had burned in a single night. Chief Nimrod and the Cushite men had checked the smoldering houses for survivors, collected lost children, and brought them into the tower.

Chief Nimrod had ordered Bab-el to stand guard over the sobbing children. The tower echoed with sobbing in a dozen different languages. Bab-el caught snippets of phrases through the buzzing in his ears. Most of them crying out in languages only Bab-el could speak. "Where's my dad?" "My arm." "I need water."

He stood all night, at the door to the tower, staring out into the fire that consumed the City of Babel. A city that had taken 10 years to build, gone in a single night. He tried to gulp down air through his tears. It was all he could do to remain standing. *This is all my fault,* he said to himself all night. Thousands of people burned alive in their homes. People he had begged to come work on the tower. People whose children were now crying behind him. Waking up from the daze only for a moment to allow a Cushite man to bring in a new child.

He didn't remember how long he stood there. Only that at one point the flames were burning into the night sky and then the sky was bright blue and the ground was billowing with dark smoke. They waited for two days for the parents to come for their children.

And some did come. But in the end there were 32 children left unclaimed. He remembered the feeling of Chief Nimrod's muscular hand painfully digging into his shoulder. His fingers smeared in black char and burns. "They say a ram with a broken leg needs larger horns," Chief Nimrod said looking at the group. Bab-el had nodded, too tired to ask what that meant.

"These children cannot be adopted by our people until they speak our languages," Chief Nimrod went on. "And you will stay inside the termite mound and teach them. And then we will decide what to do with you."

That was three years ago. Chief Nimrod had never said when he was coming back. So Bab-el began to teach the children Cushite. They were young and took to it quickly. Bab-el taught them from sunup to sundown. After class he sat at his candlelit desk late into the night, carefully translating his copy of *Adam's Scroll of Animals and Plants of Eden* for the next day's lessons. Thirty-two scrolls filled with greetings, foods, family words, plants and animals, and activities. All the Cushite, Gog, and Hebrew words the children would need to live in the Shinar valley.

It felt cathartic to copy the scrolls. Each small scroll, a container he could pour his pain into. Giving these children, as Chief Nimrod said, larger horns. And finally when his was hand too tired to keep writing, he would lay on the bed and listen to the bats crying below him, occassionally drifting into a restless sleep.

After a year the children could read and write in all the language of Shinar. As there was still no sign of Chief Nimrod. So he began teaching them Egyptian hieroglyphs. Samir was nearly fluent in Egyptian when word came that Chief Nimrod was back.

Bab-el stood alone on the roof of the tower wrapped in a blanket looking down at Chief Nimrod's massive body, now as small as an insect. Bab-el had the sudden desire to spit on him. But instead he swallowed the bitter dredges of his breakfast tea. Chief Nimrod stared up and performed a Cushite hand gesture that Bab-el interpreted as "Today is the day I kill you."

Bab-el felt like cold water had been poured down his back. He hurried down the spiral stairs. His mind raced with places he could run to. But every town he could think of had another Chief Nimrod waiting for him. He had unpaid debts to builders, kings, chiefs, and merchants in every village and city in the desert. *Maybe they need teachers on the other side of the sea*, he thought,

Bab-el rushed into his small eleventh floor room. It had been designed as an archer's lookout. But the room now held Bab-el's unmade bed, desk cluttered with quills and scrolls, and a bookshelf filled with quills and scrolls. Samir was crouched at the bottom shelf putting finger stained scrolls into a wooden bucket for class.

Bab-el took the bucket of scrolls and secured it to the dumbwaiter in the wall. It had been designed for bricks, but now only ferried class materials up and down. He gave the rope a hard tug and it slowly disappeared down the dark shaft. Then he took Samir's small hand and they walked down the long spiral staircase.

"Can we have a party after we show the elders how much we have learned?" Samir asked. Her sandals clopped cheerfully on the stairs.

"Probably not," Bab-el said his heart weighing inside his chest.

Tell her. Tell her it's your last day. Tell her how proud of her you are, his mind insisted. It was landing on him that this was the last time he would walk down these steps, the last time he would curse the builders for every uneven step he absentmindedly clipped his heel on. At one time he had meant to mark the uneven steps, but had always put it off. Three years of imprisonment had felt like forever, practically a life sentence. But here he was, walking down the stairs for the last time.

"Samir, I want to tell you something," Bab-el stammered.

"I really think people would like a party," Samir went on. "We haven't had one in a long time and Chief Nimrod coming *is* a big deal."

"Samir . . . I want to tell you that . . . today is a big day." Bab-el said.

"Ok, good! I'll go tell everyone," Samir said taking his answer and running with it.

"No. Wait, Samir!" But she had already disappeared down the circling stairs. Bab-el cursed under his breath.

He stepped down onto the ninth floor landing and stopped for a moment in front of the door. The words *Welcome to the Tower* were painted in hieroglyphs. The Egyptian floor was supposed to be the crown jewel of the tower. Something really special for shoppers who made the long climb up. It had been full of Egyptian black wigs, embalming fluids, and small golden funeral statues. It had been a rare collection, far beyond what Bab-el would have risked carrying in his days as a traveling merchant.

He took a deep breath and peeked his head inside. It smelled like bat shit and mildew. He hadn't looked inside the floors in over a year. All the Egyptian goods were gone. Thick cobwebs thatched the roof like a fog. But Bab-el noticed someone had cleared a waist-high path to one of the vendor stalls. He could see shiny rocks spread out evenly on a clean wooden counter, a little shop. Bab-el smiled at the thought of Samir trying to sell her classmates sparkly rocks.

He continued down the widening stairs. Past the ransacked farming supply floor. Past the healing center strewn with toppled pots. Past the armoury, which, last time he checked, still held an unlocked cupboard with two knives and one spear. He briefly considered hiding a knife in his robe, but he suspected that pleading to Chief Nimrod unarmed was his best chance.

Down, down he went. Until he reached the second-floor landing where he stopped at a large set of wooden double doors with the words "The Foods of the World" painted in as many languages as Bab-el knew. He could hear laughing inside. He cracked open one of the large doors and peeked inside. The large room was bustling with half-dressed kids from every shade and tribe scurrying to get ready. The floor was dotted with wooden bunk beds and kids clothes. A group of Cushite women were cleaning up spilled porridge from breakfast and navigating small arms and legs into clothes.

"Okay, this is the big day!" He heard Samir shouted with authority. "All the most *important* people in the valley will be here to see *us*! Chief Nimrod has come a long ways to see how much we learned!"

Bab-el watched, taking it all in through misty eyes. *What was Chief Nimrod going to tell them?* He wondered. *Would he bring up the fire? Tell them that Bab-el was responsible? That it was his fault their parents were dead.* He swallowed his fear, opened the door, and shouted, "Good morning, students!"

Thirty-two children and six women turned and smiled at him. "*Good morning, Papa Bab-el,*" they said in unison. First in Cushite, then in Gog, then in Hebrew, then in Egyptian. The word *Papa* felt like a punch to his gut. He felt the tears well up. He didn't want them to see him crying. They had already seen enough tears in their short lives.

"Class begins on the count of 200—" Bab-el finally said, his voice breaking.

"Get dressed!" Samir shouted in Hebrew, grabbing a small half-dressed Phoenician boy who squealed with delight. "1, 2, 3 . . ." she began to count loudly. The kids hurried to finish dressing and making their beds.

Bab-el closed the door and walked down the final set of stairs and into the large main room. The once smoke-blackened walls of the classroom were now covered with bright paint and colored phrases in various languages. "How Much?" "How Many?" "1, 2, 3, 4, 5 . . ." Pictures of flowers, mountains, birds, farmers, and a life-sized picture of Bab-el with a dozen translations of *Papa*. Looking at the picture of himself painted on the wall. *Would Chief Nimrod paint over it after he was gone?*

Bab-el walked across the large classroom to a gap in the wall where the dumbwaiter bucket sat on the floor. Bab-el lifted the basket of scrolls and began placing one scroll on each of the 32 desks he had cut with custom legs. Each leg matched the exact constellation of uneven bricks it stood on.

Bab-el sat down at his desk with his fingers steepled against his lips. He took out a fresh scroll from a drawer in his desk and drew a rough approximation of the painting. Then rolled it back up and put it in his robe.

He shouted loudly, "180, 181, 182," in Cushite. Sandals clopped down the stairs like rainfall as the children, all dressed in matching green robes and a black raven feather quill sticking out of their front breast pocket, took their seats. He nodded and smiled at each student as they sat down.

There were still two empty desks in the front of the class. "198, 199, 200." Bab-el shouted up the stairs in Egyptian. Samir ran down the stairs carrying a small girl on her back. The girl was still dressed in pajamas and wiping tears out of her red eyes.

"Sorry," Samir whispered. Her voice echoed around the room. "Mim had an *accident*." The other students sat at their desks pretending not to hear.

"Don't we have any extra robes?" Bab-el whispered as quietly as he could.

"No. The extra robes all have holes in them."

"And you wouldn't rather wear one of those?" Bab-el asked Mim.

Mim shook her head. "I want," she sniffed. "I want to get picked."

Bab-el felt his stomach twist. He looked out at his class. He could see fear peeking out behind their serene masks, many of their eyes were also red from tears. Their robes were all pressed. He could smell that they had all washed.

"Does everyone know?" Bab-el whispered to Samir louder than he meant to.

Samir nodded. "But don't worry," she smiled. "I decided I'm gonna keep living in the tower with you. We still have a lot of work to do on the storks."

Chief Nimrod must had told the Cushite matrons, he thought angrily. Bab-el rubbed his beard nervously, but he forced a smile. "Go take your seat, Samir."

Bab-el had tried to keep the adoptions a secret. He had been uncomfortable with the idea from the beginning. "How do we know they aren't going to be taken as slaves?" Bab-el had shouted at the Cushite elders. "Or sold off for the dowry?"

"We are in charge of these children." the elders had said with finality.

"I have given three years of my life to my students," Bab-el insisted.

"You owe us a lot more than three years," one of the elders had scoffed.

Bab-el stood up to address the class. But as he opened his mouth, there was a hard knock at the front door and the guard's sun-baked face leaned in. A necklace of jackal teeth rattled through the room. "The elders are here."

"Give us just a moment" Bab-el shouted nervously at the door. The students quietly glanced at each other. They had taken off their serene masks. Some were sniffing back tears. He could tell others were trying their best not to appear afraid. A few smiled with excitement. The only face of resolve was Samir's, who stood next to Bab-el's desk tapping her foot, her sandal clicking on the brick.

"As you may have already heard, the elders of the valley are coming to see how much you have learned. Three years ago—" Bab-el stopped, wishing he had written down his speech. "Three years ago the elders asked me to teach you the three languages of the valley: Cushite, Gog, and Hebrew. And I did—we did—together."

"And you have all done so well. Teaching you has been the greatest joy of my life," his voice broke off and tears again welled up in his eyes.

He took a deep breath and soldiered on. "The reason you were supposed to learn the languages is so that you would have the skills you need to live *outside* these walls." Bab-el gestured to the brightly painted walls of the classroom.

"And now you can all read *and write* in three languages, which is much more than most people you will meet." He added. "The elders will be placing you in homes. With *kind* families who will help you."

Samir raised her hand. The room went silent except for the clicking of her sandal. All eyes were on Samir. Bab-el wanted to ignore her, but he knew that it was only a matter of moments until she just shouted out her question.

"Yes, Samir?"

"My question is just for the students who are staying in the tower. What language will we be learning next?"

32 faces turned back to Bab-el. From their faces Bab-el could see that the possibility of continuing classes had not occurred to most of them.

For the students who are staying in the tower. It was a statement not a question.

"You can ask Chief Nimrod," Bab-el answered.

"Bab-el!"Chief Nimrod called from outside the door. "Bab-el, we are coming inside." Chief Nimrod's angry voice echoed through the tower and into Bab-el's bones.

Suddenly Bab-el was overwhelmed by the incredible the strangeness of it all. Ten years ago, Bab-el had parked his caravan under a palm tree outside a five-post animal-skin tent that belonged to the infamous Chief Nimrod, the man who had once single-handedly killed an elephant. The tent smelled of leather and sweat. In the center Chief Nimrod sat on a throne of elephant tusks surrounded by a dozen Cushite men in long leopard-skin robes holding wooden spears.

Bab-el had traded twenty-seven brightly colored blankets for a sliver of elephant tusk. Bab-el could have bargained for more, but he was hoping it would ingratiate Chief Nimrod for the next negotiation.

"You could trade your tusks for more lumber if you had a *Human Termite Mound* in the valley," Bab-el explained. Next to Bab-el sat a stack of red clay bricks mortared together with clay. A crudely drawn tower a drawn in the dirt. Bab-el had settled on the phrase Human Termite Mound, when he couldn't figure out the Cushite word for tower. The tent was only the height of two men, but still the tallest structure in the Shinar Valley at the time.

"And the Gogs and Hebrews also agreed to this Human Termite Mound of yours?" Chief Nimrod asked suspiciously. The three tribes that had spent generations stealing, pillaging, and burning one another's huts to the ground. But Bab-el had secured the word of the Gog council and the Hebrew elders, on the condition of Chief Nimrod's word.

"The Human Termite Mound will belong to *everyone*." Bab-el reassured him. "But, yes, the Gogs and Hebrews believe it is in their tribes' best interest to create a peaceful market. A place they can sell their goods to foreign merchants without fear of being robbed."

Bab-el had forced a smile, trying his best to look convincing. What he said was *mostly* true. Bab-el had just come from Egypt where he knew there was a high demand for the tusks and lumber.

But not high enough that most merchants were willing to risk the journey to the Shinar Valley.

"So what would you need from us?" Chief Nimrod asked fingering the point of a large tusk.

"We need you to send your best men to work on the Human Termite Mound."

Chief Nimrod sat for a long time staring at the model brick tower next to Bab-el. Then he nodded at a guard. The guard pushed the tower over and the bricks remained intact.

Chief Nimrod smirked. He nodded at a Cushite man who took two steps toward Bab-el and stuck the point of his spear up to Bab-el's throat. Bab-el tried to remain focused; it wasn't the first time he'd had a knife to his throat. He slowly raised his arms palms up.

"How do I know you aren't luring me into a trap?" Chief Nimrod said, fingering the tip of a tusk.

"I'm luring you into an opportunity," Bab-el said, glancing down at the toppled tower.

In the years of criss-crossing the desert Bab-el had pitched the tower to every king, ruler, elder, and chief he'd met. And he had never been this close.

"In Egypt, each of the Pharoahs build a massive Human Termite Mound in their honor, to remind the generations of their greatness."

Chief Nimrod leaned in closer. Bab-el continued, trying to contain his excitement. "In the far east there is a king long passed who built a wall that spans the length of the whole earth." Chief Nimrod nodded and Bab-el felt the spear's point pull away.

The next morning, Bab-el looked out at a thousand men, women, and children quietly chewing bread he had bought with the last of his life savings. Bab-el stood next to Chief Nimrod, the twelve Hebrew elders, and the Gog council.

He shouted to the crowd in all three languages,

"We, us, men and women,
will, soon, now,
build, construct, stack,
greatest, strongest, powerful,
Human Termite Mound
the valley, all the valleys, the sky,
has ever, forever, since the beginning,
seen, sight, look."

None of them, not even Bab-el, knew that two years later these villagers would all be pushed off their homeland. They would be relocated to make room for the thousands of builders pouring in from across the desert, drawn by the promise of a cut of the tower's future profits. Homes, shops, forges, and lumber mills were built on the Hebrew grazing lands. The elephants avoided the valley, scared away by the echoing of hammers and saws. The Cushite cattle were decimated to feed the builders. The Gog river was diverted in a hundred directions until it was undrinkable mud. And as the tower rose, brick by brick, the City of Babel spread across the valley like a weed.

"Welcome to our classroom!" Samir shouted to Chief Nimrod, first in Cushite, then in Hebrew, then in Gog. Her excited voice cut through Bab-el's memories. Bab-el returned to the moment to see Samir holding open the tall wooden front door, ushering in the elders of the valley. Bab-el could see that the long hunting trip had not gone well. Their faces were thin, their skin pale and ashy. Ten years ago the elders had all worn animal skins and wool robes, but now they wore thin cloaks of shiny black and gray vulture feathers.

The students all stood up and repeated the greetings. The Gog and Hebrew elders and their wives filed inside and immediately began greeting the children one by one. The looks on their faces were warm and friendly, clearly impressed that the children could now maintain conversations in their languages.

Bab-el sat at his desk watching the older students talk to the elders as their wives doted on the little ones with hugs and compliments. The room was awash in cheerfulness and friendly conversation and for a moment Bab-el thought he might not die after all.

But then Bab-el heard Samir say, "Welcome to our classroom, Chief Nimrod!"

The room fell silent. The elders and their wives gathered quietly at the front of the room behind Bab-el's desk. All eyes were on the door to the tower where Chief Nimrod stood with two large elephant tusks in his muscular arms. Bab-el felt his hope drop like a brick tumbling off the eleventh story.

"Wow! Are those *elephant* tusks?!" Samir shouted, oblivious to the change in the room.

Chief Nimrod smiled, "You speak Cushite very well for an Ethiopian." His deep voice echoed through the large room. "What is your name, girl?"

"My name is Samir. And I can also speak *and* write Hebrew, Gog, and Egyptian," she replied.

Chief Nimrod bent down and looked Samir in the eye. "That is very impressive for such a young girl. Can you speak to my Egyptian friend here?" Through the door stepped an Egyptian merchant in a gold-laced turban, a shiny vulture cloak, and a jackal tooth necklace.

"How are you, sir?" Samir said bowing deeply, as if to Egyptian royalty. "Welcome to the tower of Bab-el. I hope you will enjoy your stay." Bab-el watched from his desk, impressed that Samir remembered the lesson on Egyptian royal greetings.

"I hope so as well," the Egyptian replied. Chief Nimrod exchanged a look with the Egyptian, who nodded that he had understood Samir's words.

Chief Nimrod walked through the now silent room with an air of authority. Stopping for a moment to look at a scroll on a student's desk. Chief Nimrod greeted the elders and their wives who were lined up along the wall. And then he walked to the front of the classroom and placed the elephant tusks down on Bab-el's desk. Bab-el could smell the dust, sweat, and bird feathers.

"Move," Chief Nimrod ordered Bab-el with contempt. Bab-el stood up from his desk and slowly stepped backwards. As Chief Nimrod's eyes bored into him, Bab-el kept stepping back until he felt his shoulders bump into the brick wall. Then Bab-el realized his students were nervously watching the interaction. So he steeled his nerves as best he could, stood up straight, and nodded reassuringly at his students.

Chief Nimrod turned around and sat down in Bab-el's chair. "Children! The elders are so proud of all of you," Chief Nimrod addressed the students with a warmth and kindness that was in stark contrast to his contempt for Bab-el.

"You have learned not only the languages of the Shinar Valley, but also Egyptian! And now I have come from the far edge of the valley because I heard you have completed your studies. And I was so eager to see what you've learned! I even brought my friend Set who has come all the way from Egypt to hear children in the Shinar valley speak Egyptian." Chief Nimrod pointed to the Egyptian who stood beside him in a gold turban and bird cloak.

"So we are going to play a little game," Chief Nimrod said, rubbing the elephant tusk on the desk in front of him. "Who wants to try to sell this elephant tusk to our friend Set?" Chief Nimrod smiled at the class. There was a long painful silence in the room. None of the students raised their hands.

Chief Nimrod looked back at Bab-el with murder in his eyes. Bab-el felt sweat bead on his forehead. He scanned the room. They were all sitting quietly and trying to avoid Bab-el's eyes. *Why weren't they answering?*

Then Bab-el saw Samir at her desk in the front row. Her face was calm, but under her desk she had just unrolled a scroll with the words "Trade how much food for _____."

That was why they weren't answering. Bab-el had never taught them the Egyptian word for elephant tusk.

Bab-el discreetly took a quill from his pocket and carefully wrote the hieroglphys for "elephant tusk" and "one year's food for me" on his forearm. Samir's hand shot up.

"Ah, yes," Chief Nimrod said sounding relieved. "Samir, come up here."

Samir walked up to the Egyptian merchant and rested her hand on the creamy tusk that was larger than her entire body.

"Do you like trade one elephant tusks?" Samir said choosing one word at a time.

The merchant looked down at her impassively. "How much do you want for it?"

"Two year food for whole children," Samir said, her hand gesturing back at her fellow classmates. "Good food," Samir added. The whole class giggled. Bab-el nervously rechecked his forearm. He had written "one year's food for me."

The merchant remained stone-faced. "One year's food for the whole class. Grain for bread and two cows for milk."

Samir rubbed the tusk as if to show how smooth it was. Bab-el smiled, imagining Samir surrounded by cobwebs as she sold shiny rocks to her classmates.

"One and a half years," Samir counteroffered.

The merchant nodded. Samir turned to Chief Nimrod with her hand still on the tusk. "He wants to exchange this tusk for one and a half year's food for all the children in the tower."

Chief Nimrod narrowed his brows on Samir, and then used a series of hand gestures to re-enact the details of the trade. That's when Bab-el realized that this wasn't a game. Samir was negotiating on behalf of Chief Nimrod. She had just secured food for 32 people for a year and a half.

"Thank you, Samir. You have done very well," Chief Nimrod said, barely able to contain his excitement.

"Bab-el," Chief Nimrod yelled as he walked through the desks toward the front door. not bothering to look back at Bab-el. Bab-el took a deep breath and stepped away from the brick wall.

Bab-el paused and bent down to speak with Samir. "You did so well," he said. He felt her arms wrap around his neck. Tears rolled down his cheeks. She was still so small. He choked out the words, "You are smart and brave and you are going to do amazing things."

A tear landed on Samir's shoulder and she stepped back. "Don't worry about the other kids," she said reassuringly. "I'm gonna stay with you." And then she whispered in his ear, "And we can keep the class going, just us two, if we have to. And maybe the other kids can join us later."

He swallowed hard. He wanted to tell her he was sorry that her parents were gone, that he hoped she would grow up and make something out of the tower, or travel the world. But that most of all he wished he could be there to teach her how to use her powers for good so that she wouldn't make the mistakes he had.

"Thank you, Samir," he said wiping his checks.

As he walked through his classroom for a final time, he forced a smile at each of his students. They smiled back at him, as if hoping that Bab-el would put in a good word for them in the adoption process.

Bab-el didn't look at Chief Nimrod as he stepped outside the tower for the first time in three years. He felt hot sand pour over the edge of his sandal and onto his toes. The sky was bright blue and cloudless. He felt the hot sun and stagnant air radiating off the ground. Across the street a stork landed on a birdshit-covered rafter of the house that had belonged to one of the first tower builders. Chief Nimrod sharpened a long spear with a stone. The metal tip of the spear caught the sunlight.

"I'm sorry," Bab-el said, tears clouding his vision. "I never meant for any of this to happen. I never wanted anyone to get hurt."

Chief Nimrod said nothing. Bab-el watched the stork flutter down from its perch and land beside a muddy puddle. He really didn't want to die.

"Could you just let me go?"

"No," Chief Nimrod shook his head and continued to sharpen the blade.

"Can you at least kill me over there," Bab-el said weakly. He pointed toward the stork. "I don't want my students to have to see any more death."

After a long pause Chief Nimrod spoke. "What did that Ethiopian girl write on the scroll under her desk?" he asked coldly.

Bab-el paused and considered how much to say. "Samir didn't know the word for elephant tusk. And she didn't know how much food to ask for."

"The food was her idea, eh?" Chief Nimrod said. "How much did you tell her to ask for?"

"One year's food for herself." Bab-el said. He watched the stork drink from the muddy puddle. His own mouth felt dry.

"So how did I end up with a year and a half's food for every child?"

"Samir asked for two years," Bab-el said. "She's a smart girl." He swallowed hard. "If she has a good teacher, in a few years she could speak most of the languages in the desert."

"With a good teacher?" Chief Nimrod said finally looking at Bab-el. Bab-el felt the blade of the spear press into his neck. "Is this another attempt to *lure me into an opportunity?*"

"I'm sorry about your land. And the fire. If I could fix it I would."

"Give me your arm." Chief Nimrod demanded.

Bab-el lifted his forearm and closed his eyes, And in the darkness he heard the stork croak, *Ke Ke Ke Ke Ke Ke Ke.*

Then from a few feet away he heard Samir shouted, "CEE COO CEE COO!"

"Samir, please go wait inside," Bab-el yelled to her.

Then Bab-el felt the spear dig into his forearm. A white light of pain flashed in his mind before he passed out.

"Bab-el, Bab-el," Bab-el felt a small hand slapping his cheek. Then his eyelids were spread open.

"Are you alright?" Bab-el's eyes focused on Samir's concerned expression. He was propped up against the cool brick wall of the tower. His head ached and his forearms burned. His mouth tasted like metal. He looked down to see both his arms were covered with brown dried blood. The words *Return Him to Tower of Babel* were sliced into both his forearms, one in Cushite, the other in Egyptian.

"Where's Nimrod?" Bab-el asked.

Samir slumped down beside him in the shade of the tower. "Chief Nimrod sent the other kids home with the families. Everyone got adopted. Which is good I guess," she shrugged. "He tried to send me to live with this really old couple. But I told them that I already had plans."

He rubbed his forearms and smiled as she talked. Her voice sounded like music and he realized that she seamlessly combined words from four different languages.

"What were your plans?"

She rested her head on his shoulder. "I told them you were adopting me. Chief Nimrod argued with me about it for a really long time, but I told him we weren't done with our Egyptian lessons and that I was just learning to speak stork." Samir puffed out her chest and gave a rather convincing impression of Chief Nimrod. "And he told me to tell you that 'Bab-el better be ready to teach his Egyptian lessons tomorrow.'"

"Who's coming back to class?" Bab-el asked as he watched a few vultures perched on the ledge of a caved-in section of roof. Their heads bobbed up and down as if they were disappointed he wasn't dead.

Samir shrugged. "Did you see the stork looked up at me when I croaked. But then you shouted when Chief Nimrod started your tattoo and it flew away."

"Did you write it in the scroll?" Bab-el said painfully pushing himself to his feet. He felt lightheaded and stabilized himself on the brick wall as he walked back to the front door.

He nodded to the guard, and then heard the front door slam shut behind him. A metal lock slid into place. Samir ran across the quiet empty room, her sandals clopping against the uneven brick floor. Bab-el watched her sit down at her desk, pull out her stork scroll, and begin to write.

The people of Sodom were eating and drinking, buying and selling, planting and building, but on the day that Lot left Sodom, it rained fire.

—LUKE 17:28–29

Isaac and the Sanctuary Cities of Sodom and Gomorrah

Isaac and Ben hid in the bushes just outside town, watching a young woman hunched over a small stone well. She was struggling with the heavy rope, pulling it up hand over hand. Isaac had last sipped water before sunup, and watching her made his head ache with thirst. Finally her arms gave out and Isaac watched the rope slithered back down the well, the end laying limp in the dust at her feet. A few Canaanite men from across town burst out laughing, pointing at the young woman as they sipped from their gourds in the shade of a small inn. The woman sat in the dirt next to the well, clearly hiding herself from the men. She crossed her arms, looking determined not to let them get the best of her. Isaac knew the feeling.

"I can't believe those guys aren't helping her?" Isaac scoffed through dark dry lips.

"Really? You can't believe Canaanite men are pigs?" Ben smiled sarcastically. "But thankfully it does make our work a lot simpler." It was Ben's relentless optimism that Isaac loved most.

Ben stepped out from behind the bush and slowly sauntered down the main road. Even after two days without food Ben had an air of calm charisma. Isaac watched through the branches as Ben gestured his offer of help to the young woman. The young woman wiped her eyes and nodded gratefully. Ben had a handsome Canaanite face that tended to disarm even the most guarded people. Ben picked up the rope and slowly pulled the bucket of water out of the well, making sure not to make it seem to easy. Isaac watched as the young woman took the bucket, smiled. He took another look at the Caananite men who had returned to their conversation. They seemed to have lost interest. When she began filling Ben's gourd, Isaac stepped out onto the path.

"Isaac! What took you so long!" Ben shouted. Isaac slowly approached the two and tried to look friendly. Ben handed Isaac his gourd and Isaac took a long drink. He could feel the cool water drop all the way down his throat and pool in his gut.

"Thirsty?" Ben teased. Isaac nodded, taking another long drink.

"Rebecca, this is Isaac, my—"

"—friend," Isaac cut in. "Good to meet you, Rebecca," he said bowing in Canaanite fashion.

"So where are *you* from?" Rebecca asked her eyebrows furrowed. People always asked Isaac where he was from. He had lived in so many towns his accent was unusually muddy, which made people cautious around him.

"My family moved around a lot," Isaac continued smiling, as friendly as he could muster.

"We're on our way to Sodom," Ben said, squeezing Isaac's shoulder.

"Oh really?" the she asked, teasing.

This was exactly how they had planned it. Isaac felt the words in his throat. They were right there. *We are going to live in Sodom together.* Isaac had practiced them a thousand times. But he glanced at the Canaanite men behind her. They were eyeing Isaac and Ben suspiciously. He felt a pang in his stomach. He knew most Canaanites wouldn't care, but he lost his nerve.

"We are starting a wine business," Isaac lied, holding his smile.

"Yes . . . a wine business," Ben spoke with a flat tone, the smile fading from his face. He lowered his arm from Isaac's shoulder. Isaac looked down at the ground, ashamed of himself. Ben kept up the small talk as they filled their jugs. But Isaac could feel the fun was gone.

They walked out of town in silence, and Isaac could feel the anger radiating off of Ben. Isaac wanted to say he was sorry, that he was still getting used to being together in public. That he hadn't slept in two days. That he loved him. But the words hid in the back of his throat.

"Just one more day to Sodom," Isaac repeated to himself.

They walked all afternoon in a hot silence. Ben tried to distract himself by shooting at rodents that occassionally scurried out of the bushes and popped out of small holes in the ground. As the desert air began to cool, Ben finally shot a marmot and he laughed with delight as he picked it up by the tail.

"Water *and* dinner on the same day!" Ben smirked. Isaac laughed as the tension between them dissipated into the night.

After the sunset, Isaac built a fire and Ben dressed the marmot. They skewered the meat on long sticks and listened to it sizzle over the fire.

"I'm sorry about today," Isaac said staring into the flame. "I haven't slept since we left home." The word home brought a wave of emotion up from his stomach and he felt hot tears welling up.

"That wine business story was some of your worst work," Ben said, eating a bite of meat.

"I know," Isaac sighed.

Ben put his head on Isaac's shoulder. "Do you have any idea how wine is made?"

Isaac shrugged, his cheeks reddening.

"What if she would have asked you a question, any question?" Ben laughed. The fire crackled and sent sparks into the night sky. Isaac felt his shoulders relax at the sound of Ben's laughter.

"I was just so thirsty," Isaac sighed. "Drinking was all I could think of."

"Okay, but please don't embarrass me in Sodom. I'm not wine-businessing my way through the rest of our lives," Ben said, looking Isaac in the eyes.

Isaac nodded, "I promise."

After dinner Ben drifted off to sleep and Isaac felt the cold night settle into his bones. He wrapped himself in a blanket and fed the few remaining sticks into the fire. The crackling of the dry wood dulled the sound of Ben's snoring.

Isaac was exhausted, too tired to think clearly. His stomach twisted and turned as his mind raced with images of his father telling his mother what had happened. *Sarah, I caught your son with that Canaanite boy and the coward ran away. Your* son. He was always calling Isaac *your son.*

He tried to imagine how his mother would respond. It was hard for him to imagine them actually talking. They rarely did. They slept in different tents. Isaac rarely ever saw them together. Early in the morning, Abraham would ride his camel to the nearby town and wouldn't come home until after dark. Isaac had heard rumors that Abraham had another family in town, but he never bothered to find out. He told himself he didn't really want to know.

He poked the fire again, wondering what Abraham had told Sarah about his disappearance. *Maybe he just told her I ran away,* he thought. *Maybe he told her I was killed by thieves.* Or maybe he told his mother the truth, that he had found Ben and Isaac kissing in the field. That he had held a butcher knife to Isaac's neck until blood started to drip down. That Isaac had messed himself with fear. That Abraham had shouted at him, "If I ever catch you with that Canaanite boy I'll . . ." as he slit a goat's throat.

Or maybe he told her I took a job with some traveling merchants . . . Around and around his mind went, swirling with possible scenarios, until the first light of morning started to push the stars out of the night sky.

The sun was hot above their heads when Ben and Isaac finally saw the massive wall rising from the endless sand. The wall that surrounded Sodom was three times their height, made of smooth stones, some the size of cows.

"Look at those stones," Ben whistled as walked closer and closer. Neither of them had ever seen a walled city. Isaac imagined it must have taken several lifetimes to build.

He felt a surge of hope. *It's gonna be alright,* he repeated to himself. He smiled at the thought of this wall standing between him and his father.

Isaac had spent years waiting for this moment. Ben and Isaac had spent their youth poking and prodding their wayward sheep across hills, and no matter what they would start talking about, their conversation would inevitably wind its way back to whether they would rather live in Sodom or Gomorrah. Both Isaac and Ben had made up emphatic justifications for their prefered city, based on the scraps of information they could glean from travelers around campfires and in the marketplace.

"—but the *food* in Gomorrah," Ben would insist, having over-heard somebody use that exact phrase at a bar in town.

Isaac always wanted to live near the sea. He had once heard a traveling merchant say he "loved to watch the sun set over the Dead Sea whenever he was in Sodom." And on and on they went as they herded their sheep back down to their respective homes.

He felt an unfamiliar wetness in the air and tasted salt on the wind whipping off the Dead Sea. His heart leapt in his throat as he caught a glimpse of the sun flickering off the blue sea behind the wall. It took his breath away to see that much water. The most water he had ever seen in one place had been a waist-deep brown river lined with crocodiles.

As they neared the city Isaac could see three- and four-story clay towers peaking over the wall. They spread out in both directions as far as he could see. He noticed armored men with bows and arrows patroling the top of the wall. Isaac's feeling of excitement was replaced by an anxious twist in his stomach as he began to understand how big of a city Sodom was.

Isaac suddenly had a sinking feeling that this could all go horribly wrong. He had grown up hearing people joking about how you didn't want to get robbed by the men of Sodom. That they would steal your gold *and your manhood.* He had never taken it seriously, but seeing the large soldiers walking the walls of Sodom was making him nervous.

"If we get seperated in there, meet me under those palm trees over there," Isaac nodded at a tall green cluster of palm trees surrounded by sand. Ben nodded, trying to look like he wasn't nervous.

They finally stopped in front of a massive wooden door with timbers held together with iron, the front gate to Sodom. Isaac and Ben stood shoulder to shoulder and took a deep breath.

A soldier stepped out of a watchtower atop the wall. He looked down at them, his facial features obscured in a shadow cast by the noonday sun.

"What brings you to Sodom today?" he shouted down.

Ben shielded his eyes and squinted. He cupped his hands to shout, "We want to live here. We want to make Sodom our home."

The man pointed back and forth between them, "You two, together?"

Isaac nodded, his heart racing. "Yes," Ben shouted up.

"Alright. Leave your weapons at the gate."

"We don't have any weapons," Ben yelled, but it was lost in the loud groan of the wood and iron gates opening.

Behind the gate Isaac saw a city bathed in wild smells and colors he had never seen before. Ben and Isaac walked wide-eyed, still holding hands, silently taking it all in. They followed the man from the wall down a wide street of smooth stones.

Their guide was a dark-skinned man with an honest face named Aheb. "Sodom's reputation attracts people from all over." While Isaac wasn't sure what reputation he was referring to, the street was filled with men, women, and children of every shade walking shoulder to shoulder in robes swirling and spinning with color and texture. Isaac felt embarrassed as he fingered a hole in his dusty herding robe. Then he heard an elephant cry. He turned quickly to see a woman in a long red and gold robe riding on top of the elephant. Her hair was long and uncovered as she waved at shoppers along the side of the street. Everyone calmly moved aside as if an uncovered woman atop an elephant was just another day in Sodom.

Issac and Ben stepped into a hot bread shop to make room for the elephant. The smell of bread made his stomach pang with hunger. He ran his fingers along brightly painted pottery filled with fruits, vegetables, beans, corn, and things in shapes and colors he had no words for, each with a small sign he couldn't read.

"What is this?" Ben asked holding up a bright red fruit with a rind that flared like a flower at one end.

"That is a pomegranate," Aheb said, breaking it open and revealing clusters of red beans. Aheb offered them each one. The bean was juicy. Sweet and sour in equal parts.

"But this one isn't quite ripe," Aheb's lips puckered. "If I recognize your accent, you are from a western valley?"

Ben nodded cautiously.

Aheb nodded knowingly, waving his question aside, "You don't have to say anymore. You're welcome to share only as much as you feel comfortable."

Isaac felt his muscles relax. He realized he had let go of Ben's hand. Isaac suddenly felt lightheaded and sat down on the side of the busy street. The three days of walking and sleepless nights settled on his shoulders.

Aheb put his hand on Isaac's shoulder. "You must be tired. I will leave you here and we can finish the tour in the morning." Aheb pointed at a two-story building Isaac assumed was an inn.

Ben nodded, "Thank you, but we were planning to sleep outside the city until we can find work."

Aheb waved aside their plans, "Nonsense. As a welcome gift from Sodom your inn and meals are paid for until we can find you some work to do."

Isaac could have cried. Their own room. No more hiding out in bushes. No more making up stories. No more sneaking out after dark. They walked up the stairs to a small room with a single bed and a porch overlooking the town square. There was a side table with bread and dried meat. Isaac remembered they hadn't eaten anything since last night.

They sat on the edge of the bed eating the bread and meat in a cheerful, tired silence. Then Ben and Isaac lay next to each other on a real bed for the first time in their lives. Isaac looked into Ben's eyes and smiled. "We made it," he said reaching for Ben's hand.

"Yes, we did," Ben said. Isaac felt Ben's fingers interlock with his own. He felt his whole body sink into the bed as he closed his eyes and fell asleep.

Isaac woke up to shouting from the street. "That lightning was only a taste of what's to come for you animals!" He opened his eyes and in the morning light he saw Ben asleep next to him, his body wrapped in a blanket.

Isaac quickly dressed and walked to the small wooden balcony outside their second story room. At the center of the town square he saw a man shouting at a crowd of onlookers. "Curses fall on the wicked!" Despite the heat, the man was dressed in a long robe and gloves. Isaac couldn't see his face, but there was something concerningly familiar in the sound of his accent.

At the front of the crowd Isaac saw Aheb egging the man on. "So you're telling me that Sodom's watch tower was hit by lightning because I had sex with my husband?" Aheb shouted back. He was clearly egging the man on.

"That is only the beginning!"

"Then everyone better take cover because—" Aheb yelled as he kissed his husband to the wild cheers of the crowd. Isaac laughed, watching from the balcony.

Aheb saw Isaac standing at his balcony and waved for him to come down, "Hey, Isaac! Meet Sodom's most famous weatherman!" The shouting man turned around and Isaac's stomach twisted in terror as he recognized the man's wild eyes and long matted beard. It was his Uncle Lot. Their eyes met. Isaac lost his breath and quickly tried to step back into his room and shut the balcony curtains.

"ISAAC?!" he heard his uncle shout. He tried to think of a reasonable story, some explanation other than the truth, but his mind was blank.

"Ben, wake up," Isaac said, trying to keep his voice low. "Please, wake up." Ben was still snoring, his body wrapped in the sheets. Isaac shook him. "Wake up!" His heart was pounding and he felt short of breath.

There was a hard knock. "Isaac? Isaac, are you in there?" Lot shouted through the door.

Ben rolled awake. "What's going on?" his voice groggy.

Isaac frantically looked for somewhere to hide. The room only had a bed and a small table. He glanced at the balcony and for a moment seriously considered risking the two-story jump. Then he remembered the stone street below.

"Isaac! Were you kidnapped?!" Lot yelled through the door. "I'm gonna break down the door!"

Ben saw the fear in Isaac's eyes and tucked the bed sheet around his waist. "Who is that?" he whispered.

Isaac threw Ben's robe at him. "It's my uncle. Hide under the bed," Isaac whispered forcefully. Ben put on the robe, rolled off the bed, and hid under it.

Isaac took a deep breath and Isaac opened the door a crack. "No, Uncle. I'm fine." Isaac said barely concealing the defeat in his voice.

"What are you doing here?" Lot frantically whispered close to the crack in the door. His beard was matted and cracked lips glistened with sweat and sand. His uncle looked wild-eyed, almost unhinged. Standing on the stairs behind him, Isaac saw two small girls, who had a striking resemblance to his uncle. They were both holding tanned cow hides decorated with paint. One had a large crude drawing of a lighting bolt and what he assumed was the city of Sodom on fire. The other girl had a sign with two men kissing, both engolfed in flames.

Isaac felt his stomach twist. He stared down at the drawings held by his small cousins, then back up at his Uncle Lot. Isaac hadn't seen him in years and didn't know what he would do if he found Ben under the bed.

"I . . . I . . . I . . ." Isaac stumbled. Lot pushed the door open with his shoulder and grabbed Isaac's face with his leather gloves. "Did they hurt you?" Lot whispered with vitriol. Isaac could feel his hot breath on his ear. "I won't let those dogs lay a finger on you." His face was nearly touching Isaac's.

"I . . . I . . . came to visit you," Isaac said, forcing a smile.

"Did you come with anyone?" Lot said, his eyes darting around the room.

Isaac shook his head. "No," he lied.

"We need to get you out of here." Lot grabbed Isaac by the wrist and led him out of the room. Lot lifted his daughters on each of his shoulders. "It's not safe for a young man like you to be walking the streets," he said, pulling Isaac down the stairs.

Isaac walked in a sickening daze out of the inn and followed his uncle into the streets of Sodom. "Stay back!" His uncle snarled at a few onlookers, "Keep your hands off him!" Isaac's eyes stared down at the cobblestone street. Ashamed of his uncle, desperately hoping Ben didn't try to follow him. Isaac didn't look up as he drifted behind his uncle back through the massive wooden gates that led out of Sodom. There were two camels tied to palm tress just beyond the wall. Isaac mounted one of the camels and rode behind his uncle and two cousins in a heavy silence. Isaac watched the cluster of palm trees fade into the desert behind him, trying to remember the way back to Sodom.

That night, Isaac sat silently stared at his dinner as Lot and his wife, Ado, yelled at each other.

"I told you to *leave* our daughters out of it." Ado yelled. The two girls didn't look up from their dinner, their fingers and shirts covered in rice and greasy goat meat.

"They *wanted* to come!" Lot smiled at his daughters. "They made the signs themselves! Didn't you girls?" Isaac watched under the table as his cousin's four legs happily dangled off their stools. Their faces calm, as if nothing was happening. He remembered eating dinner with his parents, the suffocating silence between Sarah and Abraham filling the tent.

"That isn't the point!" Ado scoffed. "They are *my* children and I'm not gonna let you use them like some prop."

"*Prop!*" Lot threw up his hands. A glistening leg of goat meat in one hand and a fistful of bread in the other. "Those animals—"

"Those *people*," Ado cut him off, "have allowed us to live outside their city, given us access to their water and someday our daughters will—" There was a hard knock at the front door.

Isaac instinctively put his hand on his knife. The girls' legs stopped swinging and they looked at the door. Lot leaned in and put his finger to his cracked lips, "Shhh."

Lot quietly stood up and opened the door a crack. Isaac could see dozens of flaming torches outside.

Lot slammed the door and put his back against the door as a barricade. "They finally worked up the balls to burn down my house," he said, his face white with fear.

"We are here to get Isaac!" Aheb's voice shouted from outside the door.

Lot yelled through the closed door with derision, "Well you'll have to find someone else to have your way with!"

"We're not leaving without him!" Ben shouted. Isaac's heart leapt to his throat. *Get up. Get up.* He told his legs. *This is your chance. Just walk out the door and leave.* But Isaac's legs didn't move.

Lot was gaining confidence and maniacally shouted back, "I have two daughters, but you wouldn't be interested in them would you?!"

"*Are you insane?*" Ado whispered angrily.

Lot put his finger to his lips and smiled, "Shhh."

Ado stood up enraged and wiped off her daughter's greasy fingers on her skirt. Then she lifted the two girls onto her hips and left the room.

Isaac felt sick watching his uncle muttering to himself, like he was steeling his nerves for a fight.

Isaac stared across the room at the window. He imagined himself throwing his chair at Lot and escaping out the window. But then he thought about his parents. Lot would tell them he had gone with the boys of Sodom. Issac saw his mother's face twisted in disgust. "My only son," she would sob. Isaac tried to string together *some* explanation that would convince his mom that running away to Sodom wasn't exactly what it looked like.

"Let him out!" Ben shouted though Isaac's thoughts. Isaac could hear the tears in Ben's voice.

Isaac felt years of frustration welling up inside him. He was supposed to be eating dinner with Ben, sipping wine, and laughing with their new friends. Finding ripe pomegranates and riding elephants. And yet here he was, a stone's throw from Sodom with his sweating uncle pushing his full weight against the door.

He was sick of lying and hiding and making up stories. He was going to find Ben and they were going to run away to Gomorrah. And if that didn't work, they would build a hut in the middle of a desert.

When it was finally quiet. Lot opened the door a crack. Outside Isaac could see torches disappearing back into the darkness. Lot sat back down, dabbing his forehead with the sleeve of his robe.

For the rest of the meal, Isaac sat in stoic silence, listening to the sound of Lot's jaw mash his dinner. The sound fueled the anger inside him.

"Not hungry?" Lot said between bites. Isaac didn't answer.

"Spending a night in that city would make anyone lose their appetite," Lot nodded, wiping the sweat beads off his brow.

"I sent word to Abraham telling him you made it here safe," Lot said, eyeing his goat leg for more meat. "I told him to come get you. As you can see it's just not safe for young men in these parts," Lot scoffed. Isaac's stomach lurched and he felt his chest tightening with panic.

"I . . . I think I'll head to bed," Isaac said much too loudly. He cleared his throat and slowly stood up, forcing himself to casually walked out the back door of the house. Outside he stood in the dark wondering how close his father was. Was he already on his way? He should have asked his uncle when he expected him. He imagined Ben sitting under the cluster of palm branches waiting for him. The words, *Let him out!* repeated over and over in Isaac's mind.

Isaac closed the door to the guest room. He sat down on a small child's bed, watching the lights in the house slowly snuff out. Then he got up and snuck outside. Clouds obscured the glow of the moon and Isaac walked slowly around the dark house. Watching the ground, making sure he didn't step on any branches. He made his way slowly to the front of the house. The camels were gone. He was sweating nervously. He focused his eyes on the sand under his feet, looking for the path back to Sodom. He saw the clusters of footprints outside the front door. There were camel prints interspersed but they seem to go off in every direction and it was too dark to see a pattern. He got down on his hands and knees. He wouldn't make it. Not on foot. He heard a few camels braying from the darkness. But he was worried he would wake someone up if he tried to mount one.

He went back to the bedroom and lay down on the childsized bed, his feet hanging off the end. He thought of Ben sitting under the palm trees wondering how long he would wait for him.

Isaac woke to the braying of camels and roosters calling in the gray morning light. He got dressed and sat outside and watched the sun rise over Sodom. He imagined himself walking down the street, the smell of fresh bread and wild fruits, walking hand in hand with Ben.

"Isaac," his Aunt Ado's voice interrupted his thoughts. "Come help me milk the camels." She had a tall clay jar in her arms. "If you're going to stay here, you're going to pull your weight." Behind her a few camel's necks were craning over the side of a fence and eating the dusty leaves off a browning bush.

Isaac followed her into the camel pen feeling like he was back in his old life. *Old life?* he thought. He had only spent one day in Sodom. Ado separated a calf from her mother with the click of her tongue. The calf trotted to the far end of the pen and Ado placed the jar under the mother. Isaac started to milk the camel.

"There you go." Isaac said letting the camel smell his hand. When Ado looked away, Isaac took a handful of shit and wiped it across the backside of the camel. Marking it for later.

"Do you want help cleaning the storeroom?" Isaac asked.

Lot met his brother Abraham in the shade of a rocky overhang just beyond the view of the watchman walking the walls of Sodom.

"How many people *have* you cured of this disease?" Abraham asked from atop his camel. Lot stood in the shade below, drinking water from a gourd before handing it to Abraham.

"Not one," Lot scoffed.

Abraham looked down at Lot. His eyes filled with derision. "You have been here for all these years and you haven't found one?"

"They're getting bolder. They tried to burn my house down last night." Lot paused for effect. "They were going to rape your son." Lot sneered wiping the sweat off his forehead with his sleeve.

Abraham tightened his grip on the reigns. Lot could feel anger radiating off his brother. "This disease is spreading across the desert. Men in my valley have been found *together*." Abraham sneered in disguist.

Abraham took a long drink of water from his gourd. "Adam burned his garden to the ground in order to protect his family from snakes," Abraham said, clicking his tongue. His camel began slowly walking toward Sodom, and Lot followed closely behind.

Isaac sat on the small bed, tapping his foot in anticipation. He sat on the bed staring out the window as the sun set over Sodom in the west. The clouds were a fluffy array of orange and purple. He nervously rechecked his leather satchel: beans, flour, milk, a change of clothes, and rope from the storeroom. He had everything they needed for the three days' ride to Gomorrah. He hated waiting. He always wanted to wing it, but Ben would insist on a plan, getting their stories straight for a third time.

He had spent the day between the house and the storeroom gathering supplies and avoiding Ado who seemed to be watching him around every corner. She had nearly caught him marking the main path back to Sodom. Isaac had been going back and forth with himself all day about when to leave. Lot had left in the morning and Ado didn't know when he was due back. In the end Isaac had decided to wait until dark.

The camel brayed down at Isaac through the window. He had tied her up behind his room and Isaac sensed that she wanted to get back to her calf.

"Shh." Isaac hushed her quickly, grabbing another handful of rock salt from his satchel and offering it up. He felt the camel's dry, coarse tongue on his palm.

"You miss your baby," Isaac whispered as he scratched her cheek. Isaac thought of his own mother. Maybe she was on her way right now. He would have liked to have a few moments alone with her before he left, but he was sure Abraham would never have let her come alone.

Isaac watched the blinding orange sun fall behind the placid sea. With the sun gone he noticed wisps of smoke rising over the outer walls of the city. Clusters of little cooking fires. But then the plumes widened into dark gray pillars. All across the the wall ominous dark pillars rose up. Isaac had seen similar billows when he watched a forest burn. He put his satchel over his shoulder, opened the door a crack, and checked the graying light for sign of Ado and the girls. They were inside eating dinner.

He grabbed the camel's reigns and made his way around the guest house, crouching low out of the view of Ado. He pulled the camel through the homestead and into the bushes. The camel let out a loud cry.

"Shh," Isaac whispered, yanking on the reigns.

"Isaac!" Ado shouted from the house. The camel bucked at the sound of Ado's voice. Isaac's heart raced. His hands shook as he pulled out a handful of rock salt from his satchel. The camel slowly ate it and Isaac rubbed its snout soothingly. He mounted the camel and clicked his tongue. As the camel trotted out of the bush onto the path to Sodom he heard Ado shout at him, "Stop!" She shouted again, "Stop that thief!"

Isaac looked back at her. She was pointing at him and screaming for someone to stop him. Isaac scanned the bushes along the path, half expecting Lot to come racing after him. But nobody came. There was no one to help her. Their house sat alone on a hill far beyond earshot of any of the people of Sodom. Isaac galloped out of the homestead, glancing back to see his cousins still seated at the dinner table.

Isaac rode down the path to Sodom in the gathering darkness, the cool salty air beginning to reek of smoke and ash. The smoke towering over the city enveloped the last of the purple sky and Isaac could finally see the entire city was ablaze. He whipped the camel to ride faster as the cold, charred wind bit into his sweating arms. His hands ached from holding the reins white-knuckled.

He thought of Ben trapped in the small room. The fire consuming the inn. A pain shot through his stomach as he imagined Ben jumping from their balcony and breaking his legs on the street below. Screaming for help as people ran in every direction.

He whipped the camel again, pushing her to ride faster. Soon the red glow lit up the night sky. As he rode down the sandy trail he began to see clusters of people gathered outside the city walls. He slowed to a trot as he approached the first cluster. The children were crying, the three women had their arms around as many children as they could reach.

Isaac got down from the camel and walked through the crowds. There were thousands of people. Some huddled together talking quietly, a few just staring at the towering flames in disbelief. The massive wooden gates hung charred as flames ran up them. People were staggering out of the door in twos and threes.

Isaac scanned the walls until he found the palm tree. The leaves were blowing back and forth, untouched by the flames. He pulled the camel through the denser and denser crowd of people, his heart racing, his mind swirling with what he would do if Ben wasn't there. He would ride into the fire. He would search every street. He would rather burn with Sodom.

Then he saw Ben leaning next to the trunk of the tree. Ben's back was to the fire as he stared out into the dark toward Lot's house. Isaac's heart unclenched and he felt warm tears well in his eyes. "Ben!" he shouted. "Ben!"

Ben looked away from the dark and their eyes met. Ben smiled wide and ran toward him. Isaac felt Ben's arm wrap tightly around him, his body warm and solid. "I was waiting for you," Ben whispered in Isaac's ears. "I went to that maniac's house but you weren't there and I was worried he had murdered you or something."

"I tried to come find you, but I then I got lost in the dark," Isaac said, his tears tumbling onto Ben's bare shoulder.

Ben pulled back and held Isaac's shoulders. "The whole city is burning. Some people are talking about waiting here and seeing what is left in the morning. I heard some others are planning to go to Gomorrah at first light."

Isaac felt the the leather reins in his hand. "I want to leave," Isaac insisted. He wanted to leave before Lot came looking for him.

Ben nodded in agreement. "It's a two days' ride to Gomorrah."

Isaac could hear a few men nearby who were talking loudly, as if they were taking charge. He watched them for a moment, pointing where the nearest wells were, how the fire was spreading, where it was dying down. A few were already discussing plans for rebuilding.

"Hold this for me," Isaac said, handing the camel reins to Ben.

Isaac slapped his cheeks a few times till they felt red, then he walked back a few paces into the crowd. He waited for a moment and then burst out of the crowd at a sprint, running right up to the men panting.

"Have you seen my friend Isaac?" Isaac asked urgently.

The men shook their heads. "Nobody named Isaac," one man said. They nodded to each other, pained looks of commiserative grief on their faces. Isaac's shoulders slumped as if he was stricken by grief. "He was with that maniac Lot and, and, and he ran back into the fire and I didn't see him come out!"

"We'll watch for him, son," one of the men said, leaning over and putting a reassuring arm around Isaac.

"Thank you," Isaac said, forcing his voice to falter.

Isaac turned and slowly walked away from the men who stood in a respectful silence.

Isaac walked back to Ben, and when they were close enough to whisper Ben leaned in, "I love you." Isaac flashed a smile, took Ben's hand, and together they disappeared into the crowd.

The person to be cleansed must wash their clothes, shave off all their hair and bathe with water, then they will be ceremonially clean. After this they may come into the camp, but they must stay outside their tent for seven days. On the seventh day they must shave off all their hair, they must shave their head, their beard, their eyebrows and the rest of their hair. They must wash their clothes and bathe themselves with water, and they will be clean.

—LEVITICUS 14:8–9

Doctor Leviticus

Dinah clicked her tongue and pulled on the reigns. Dinah's sword sheath clanged against her dusty thigh armor as her camel came to a stop. Before her stood a wooden fence surrounding a complex web of gardens with a sign that read *Welcome to Doctor Leviticus' Office.*

"Levi!" Dinah shouted from atop her camel. "Come say hi to your sister Dinah!"

A bald head popped up from behind the fence. Dinah gasped in surprise and instinctively reached for the handle of her sword. Then she noticed the bald head belonged to a woman with kind eyes, ruddy wrinkled cheeks, and no eyebrows. Dinah relaxed and moved her hand away from the sword.

"Doctor Leviticus?" the woman asked, correcting Dinah.

"Possibly. The person I'm looking for just goes by Levi," Dinah said cautiously. She couldn't help staring at the older woman's sun-baked forehead where her eyebrows should have been. Then Dinah saw two more bald, eyebrowless women rise from behind a berry bush. Both held watering cans and looked at her suspiciously.

"I didn't know Doctor Leviticus had a sister," the older woman smiled, pointing at a two-story brick building with stairs that wound along the outer walls. On the second floor was a door flanked by large lattice windows and closed curtains.

A few chickens ran up and down the paths that cut across the maze of lush green gardens. Dinah had been on the road for a month and was impressed to see a garden this green in the middle of the drought.

Dinah dismounted her camel and her sword clanged against her armor. She made a move to push open the short wooden front gate.

The older woman pulled a linen face mask over her nose and mouth and blocked the gate with her body.

"You can't come in like *that!*" the woman shouted, scandalized.

"Why not?" Dinah asked, her eyebrows narrowing on the woman on the other side of the wooden gate.

"Because you're unclean!" the woman exclaimed through her linen face mask. She pointed at the small one-room mud hut on Dinah's side of the fence. A sign above the door read *Washroom*.

"I've been on the road for a month," Dinah said getting irritated. "Levi's not going to care."

"He most certainly will care," the woman scolded Dinah. "You are unclean and you could contaminate everything in here." The woman's hands made a circular motion that encompassed the building and its gardens.

"So you want me to wash *before* I come in," Dinah said, pointing at the washroom. The washroom it was empty save for three wooden buckets full of clear water and a series of strangely labeled bottles.

The bald woman smiled and nodded, "Please."

"Can I just talk to my brother," Dinah was getting impatient. Then she saw the second-floor curtains move and a moment later her brother's bald head flashed through a gap in the fabric.

"LEVI!" Dinah shouted to him, pushing the gate and the woman out of her way.

And a moment later her brother hurried out of the door and scurried down the stairs, waving his arms frantically. "Dinah wait, WAIT!" he yelled as he ran. Dinah stood still, the gate half open.

Dinah barely recognized her brother Levi. He wore a bright white linen bathing robe tied around his thin and bony frame. A linen face mask covered his sallow face. His dark, long hair and eyebrows were gone. Dinah felt disoriented by the bony, pale shell of her oldest brother. Three years ago, Levi had left their father Jacob's house a well-built man with a plump wife and a healthy baby. But no one in the family had heard from Levi since. Their father Jacob had finally sent her to check-in on Levi.

"It's good to see you, Dinah," he said, breathing heavily through the face mask. He pushed the front gate against her metal chest plate. The latch clinked shut.

"Good to see you too, Levi," Dinah said concerned.

"Could you . . ." he caught his breath, "do me a favor and please wash off and change before you come in."

"You want me to change *before* I come in," she said flatly.

"I just . . ." Levi stood in front of her as if trying to find the right words. "Well, just to be safe." He paused again. ". . . I'm trying to keep things in here clean." His pale bon,y fingers motioned toward the brick building. Perhaps Levi sensed this wasn't sitting well with his sister because he added, "The plague has already taken so much from these woman."

Dinah had seen the effects of the plague. She had spent a month riding through village after village emptied of all but the stench of rotting bodies. Sometimes she rode for days seeing nothing but empty houses along the road, yards strewn with toys, farming tools, and dead bodies. Whole villages had died before anyone could bury the dead. When someone came down with a fever they could be gone the very next day.

"What do you want me to change into?" Dinah said, looking down at her dust coated armor.

Levi smiled and looked quite relieved. He clapped his bony, hairless hands together. "Excellent! There should be three buckets of fresh water and a clean bathing robe in the washroom," he pointed at the small hut. "You can use the first bucket to wash your clothes and armor. The second bucket to wash your whole body. And the third bucket to shave off your hair and eyebrows."

Dinah pulled off her dirt and sweat-stained headwrap.

"You want me to shave off *all* my hair?" She tried to shake out her long, brown, and very tangled hair.

Levi nodded at her, his eyes pleading.

"And my eyebrows," he nodded again. "Just to keep your house clean? Where are Adina and Merari?" Dinah asked looking around, hoping that Levi's wife would step in and save her hair.

"They're gone," Levi said, looking past her, his voice quiet and distant.

"Gone where?" Dinah said, a sense of dread landing like a rock in her stomach.

"They died forty-seven days after we got back from our father's house," he said.

"Levi, I'm—" Dinah felt tears welling in her eyes.

Levi's shoulders fell, the wind knocked out of him. "Please, at least wash the fleas out of your hair."

She stood in the washroom scrubbing her head with a liquid from a jar labeld "Fleas." It smelled like citrus and herbs. As she ran her fingers through her hair she noticed a tiny black flea on her finger. She ran her fingers through her hair again. It was only the one flea. She stared at it. It was far too small for Levi to have seen.

Dinah stood in her brother's office in a long bright-white bathing robe, her hair wrapped in a towel. She had met village healers before, but this was something different. The office walls were covered in shelf after shelf of scrolls. The floor was dotted with various sized clay jars with labels like "Milk thistle," "Mountain plum," "Flax," and "Garlic oil." She opened the lid of a tall jar on the floor with a label that read "Day Two." Inside small pink flower petals floated on top of olive oil. The room filled with a sweet floral smell.

Each shelf was labeled with the name of a family with a dozen or more scrolls perfectly stacked on each shelf. She unrolled a scroll marked, *Family of Gidioni*. Inside it read:

> *Gidioni, husband of Yehudit, father of Abidan*
> *Yehudit said her husband Gidioni was sick with the fever for two weeks. Possible causes: eating an ostrich egg, eating elderly camel meat, bearing a grudge against*

his neighbor for stealing his ax, sleeping with Ada during menstruation, green spots of mold on the walls of their house.

Treatment
Shave off all body hair, wash all bodies three times each day, wash the entire house and lock it up for seven days and sleep in a tent. One for Gidioni and one for rest of the family. Reconcile with your neighbor. Begin clean diet. No sex during menstruation. Wash sheets after sex.

She re-read the scroll, trying to understand it. Why had her brother had become so fixated on washing? And what was a clean diet? She heard her brother coming and quickly put the scroll back on the shelf.

Leviticus walked up the circular stairs and offered her a plate of olives and flatbread. "What is all this?" Dinah asked, taking a handful of olives and a bite of flatbread.

"My research," Levi said as he sat down on a tall leather chair behind the desk. "So how is our family?" he asked as he straightened the quills on his desk. "I was disappointed to have missed Joseph's birth celebration. But I was so busy with patients. The sickness has hit our village hard."

Dinah cautiously followed his redirection, "Everyone is well. Our brother's spend sunup to sundown watering in the fields. Dad hardly leaves the house. He spends all day doting over baby Joseph. Mom keeps talking about moving to Egypt, but Dad isn't having it. Says he wants all his kids raised in the country."

Levi pulled the curtain open slightly with his fingers. The afternoon sun shone off his bald eyebrowless head.

Levi flicked the curtain shut. Then he stood up and washed his hands. He opened the tall jar of olive oil and placed a drop on his right earlobe and right big toe. He did it without thought. As if it was perfectly normal. Dinah watched the strange ritual in silence.

"Levi, are you sure you're alright?" she asked.

He looked out through the curtains. "Yes. I'm just fine," he said, forcing a smile. "My next patient is waiting for me. You should get some rest in the guest house. We can talk more tonight over dinner." He opened the door and motioned for her to leave the office.

Outside, Dinah saw a bald woman waddling through the front gate, her head was still red from being freshly shaved. She had a wet chicken in her hands. "What is going on?" Dinah said to herself.

While the bald patient was in the office with Levi, Dinah decided to complete her training for the day. "Neck, side, gut . . ." she repeated to herself as she dogged, blocked, and thrust her sword straight ahead into an imaginary soldier. She occasionally caught the three bald woman staring at her, but they quickly returned to pulling weeds when she glanced in their direction.

She stopped training when her brother walked out of his office. He made his way down the stairs with a piece of linen covering his mouth. He was trailed by the plump woman with the squawking chicken and a small jar marked "Fever oil" in her hands.

Levi walked across the yard to a small fire that had been burning since Dinah arrived. He took the chicken and plunged it into a bucket of water three times. Then he slit the throat with a small knife. The chicken flopped and jerked as he held it upside down until all the blood had drained into a small fire. Then he cut it open the chicken and began pulling out each organ.

Levi turned each small wet organ in his hands. Checking every part of the stomach, lungs, and heart before washing them in a separate bucket and casually tossing them into the small fire.

It was the strangest butchering process Dinah had ever seen. She planted her sword in the dirt and walked over to the fire. "Why are you washing the organs if you're just gonna toss them in the fire?" Dinah asked, entranced with her brother's meticulous care.

"You have to check the organs," he said, and the bald woman nodded knowingly.

"Check them for what?" Dinah asked.

"Irregularities," Levi said, rolling a handful of small intestines through his fingers before throwing it into the fire. Then he began lancing each piece of pink chicken meat to a spit and laying them over the fire.

It was late in the afternoon when the woman left his house with the jar of fever oil and most of the roasted chicken. "Don't go back into your house before the seventh day!" Levi reminded her as she waddled out the front gate.

"Okay, let's wash up and eat," Levi said to Dinah and called the three women still weeding in the garden.

"What was all that about?" Dinah asked, taking a bite of blackened chicken.

"Her husband has the sickness and she's trying to take care of him." Levi shook his head, "It's a shame. She's such a sweet woman."

"Do you think he'll be alright?" Dinah asked.

"No. It's too late for him. But she might survive if she washes and leaves him alone," he took a bite of chicken. "But they never do."

After dinner Dinah sat on her bed writing a letter to her father by candle light. She wrote that she had made it safely. That Adina and Merari had died and that Levi was—she paused searching for the right word—grieving. That she needed to stay and look after him for a while. "Levi and I send our love to you and the family."

In the morning, she woke up to the rooster crow in the cold gray of the morning. She fastened her cold metal chest plate, shoulder armor, wrapped her face and hair, and mounted her camel.

The sun was already hot overhead as she approached the small town. She rode slowly past a cluster of women seated on blankets as they shouted the prices of small browned vegetables that buzzed with flies. Behind the women, children ran and played in a dirt field.

Dinah noticed two women with shaved heads and no eyebrows who were weaving baskets together a short distance away from the rest. No one seemed to be buying any of their vegetables.

"Hey, girlie, you like playing with swords?" someone cat-called. Dinah gripped the handle of her sword and turned to see a man in spotless armour and a small crown. He was thrusting his erect sword in the air and smirking at her. Next to him, four soldiers sat on the shade of a restaurant's small porch.

Dinah was used to men shouting at her. She did her best to look like she hadn't heard them while also staying vigilant of their movements.

"I said, 'Hey, girlie,'" the prince whistled at her. She kept riding without looking at him. Then the prince stumbled in front of the camel. "Hey, where you going so fast?" he smirked. "I don't have a *soldier* wife yet. You want to be a princess?" his erect sword pointed at her.

Dinah clicked her tongue and her camel picked up pace down the main street.

At the far end of town she found a small shop for sending letters. Beside the shop a few boys used rags on sticks to wash dusty camels nearly twice their height. Dinah placed her letter on the counter.

"I need to send this to Jacob in Bethel." The shopkeeper looked up from her writing. Her face was wrinkled and leathery, and Dinah noticed she didn't have any eyebrows.

"Did you by chance go to see my brother, Levi?" Dinah asked, unsure if there were other doctors in town who also shaved their patients' eyebrows.

The shopkeeper's face softened as if suddenly they were friends, "Oh, I didn't know Doctor Leviticus had a sister."

"I'm visiting him for a few weeks," Dinah smiled, quickly pulling a few coins out of her pocket.

"No, no, no, your money's no good here," she waved Dinah off. "Any family of Doctor Leviticus is on the house." She took Dinah's letter and whistled at one of the boys washing the camel. "This one goes to Bethel. *Right* away." She tossed the boy the letter.

She turned back to Dinah, "I've *tried* to pay Leviticus for all he's done for my family. But he *insisted* that he wouldn't take any money. All he asked for was one chicken." The shopkeeper laughed to herself, "He even sent me home with most of the meat."

"Levi, I mean Leviticus, always was generous," Dinah smiled.

"Sorry about the prince. He's been like that since he came to town."

Dinah flashed a smile before asking, "So he really is a prince?"

"He says he is. He's asked all the women in town if they wanna be a princess," she scoffed. "He'll probably find someone. A lot of widows are just looking for someone to take care of their children."

"Thanks for sending the letter," Dinah said. She pulled her headscarf over her mouth and mounted her camel. As she rode past the prince he whistled at her and shouted, "Come back again sometime!"

That night Dinah sat around the crackling fire, polishing her armor and laughing. "Wait, so you think people's hair is making them sick?" she teased her brother.

"Well your hair had fleas, so . . ." he smirked and took a long drink of water.

"One flea. I had one flea," Dinah laughed. "I can't believe you saw that."

Levi shrugged, "I didn't see it. I just figured since you had been on the road a long time. But generally, bald people do live longer."

"You mean people who live longer are bald," she smiled.

"Both," Levi pointed up to his office. "I have a hundred examples on those scrolls."

It felt good to laugh with him. Despite all his physical changes his light hiccuping laugh was exactly how she remembered it.

"So why not eat pigs?" Dinah asked.

"Have you seen what a hungry pig will *eat*? I once watched a pig eat an entire human carcass in one sitting." Levi shivered with disgust.

"Okay, fine. But camel meat? I mean, I've been eating it my entire life. And look at me." Dinah made a show of flexing her arms.

"So my theory is this. Camels are fairly valuable around here. So people don't tend to eat them until the camel is old or sick."

"Why not tell people not to eat old, sick camels?" Dinah asked, leaning in and pointing at her brother.

"Fair point, but I'm beginning to suspect that there is something about animals that chew their cud that makes them safer for eating."

"What?" Dinah rolled her head back and let loose a belly laugh. And the more she thought about it the harder she laughed. "Okay, okay," she said, wiping the tears from her eyes. "Whew."

Then she saw her brother was sitting upright in his chair, his arms crossed and his face hardened. She had gone too far.

"Alright, I'm sorry, Levi," she said and took a few deep breaths. "I want to understand, but it's just *so strange.*"

His face softened, changing from Doctor Leviticus back to her brother, Levi. He leaned forward with four fingers up. "Okay from what I can tell, it comes down to four things that I suspect make people sick. Blood, Dirt, Death, and Anger. People get sick when they eat blood—"

"And menstruate," Dinah added with a wry smile.

"Yes, that too," Levi nodded.

"I've also started noticing that the people who die have had contact with someone or something who died. You always see vultures when people are sick."

"And washing seems to help. Keeping the dirt away is important." He brushed off his hands. "It's also why circumcision—"

"Yeah, I don't need to hear the details on that," Dinah shook her head.

"And lastly, I found that sickness often hits homes where there is some kind of anger or unresolved conflict."

"Because maybe they get *murdered* by the person who's mad at them?" Dinah started giggling again. She tried to cover her mouth. "I'm sorry. It's just . . ."

"Laugh all you want," Levi said, dismissing his sister's laughter. The was a hint of defiance in his voice. "But I'm keeping people alive. The women that live here, their families are *all* dead from the sickness. They came to stay here with me. And we have not lost one person." His index finger was raised.

Dinah remembered Adina and Merari and her stomach suddenly twisted with embarrassment. She stared into the fire, feeling her face blush. She remembered seeing Levi holding hands with Adina as they left her house. Levi had looked so happy.

"I'm sorry. I shouldn't laugh," she said.

"When Adina and Merari got sick I didn't have any rules," he sighed. "It was actually their sickness that started my research. I started writing everything down. Everything they ate and drank, every herb I gave them, when they went to the bathroom, what they threw up, what it looked like."

"Then I started interviewing people in town to see what treatments were working. By the time Adina died I had a scroll for everyone in town."

Dinah stared into the fire. "Why didn't you tell us they died?"

Levi didn't answer for a long time. "Enough about all that. Tell me about how you became a soldier," he nodding toward her armor.

Dinah looked at her half-polished armor, dully reflecting the flames. "I guess I just like it," she shrugged. "The boys were always working out in the field and Father would tell me to stay home and watch over the house. Then I figured I should be able to do something more than just *watch* our house get ransacked by robbers."

"From what I can see you're pretty good with a sword." Levi smiled at her. "The office could use a security guard." His face was pale and gaunt, but his smile was the same.

"I missed you, Levi," Dinah smiled back at him.

"I missed you too, Dinah." He poked the flames with a long stick, sending amber sparks up into the dark night sky.

Dinah quickly fell into a routine with her brother. As long as she was there to greet and collect water for the patients, Levi mostly left her to her own devices. She used her new freedom to train. She got up before dawn. Her armor clanged and woke the roosters as she ran up and down the hills surrounding Levi's office.

She spent her afternoons attacking a wooden scarecrow she attached to the fence behind her bedroom. As she trained, Levi met with patients or worked alongside the women in the garden. Kneeling on a blanket as he clipped the leaves from herbs or weeded around his flowers. He never interrupted her training except to let her know that they could use more water from the river, "When she had a moment."

But as the drought wore on more and more villagers came down with the sickness. And eventually the nearby homesteads were mostly empty. Nearly everyone in town had died or relocated to Egypt. The few people who were left spent most of their days lined up along the fence, waiting to see Doctor Leviticus.

Eventually there was no one healthy enough to actually go into Levi's office. Dinah and the three women spent their mornings carrying buckets of water back and forth from the river. Watering the vegetables and handing out cups of water to the dying men and women who camped in the ditch along the fence.

Levi, on the other hand, never left his office. He was frail and tired. He washed his hands over and over again. He hardly slept. He spent day and night filling scroll after scroll with the genealogies, diets, and living habits of his dying patients. He stopped leaving his office. Day after day he asked Dinah if there were any patients healthy enough for him to see.

"Well, what am I supposed to tell them, Levi?" Dinah shouted at him, pacing back and forth in his office. Her eyes were tired and her bald and eyebrowless head was browned from months under the unrelenting sun. "Levi, these people are sick and desperate." She dabbed olive oil on her right earlobe. The action had become second nature during her time at Levi's.

"Help us!" a woman shouted. Levi winced in pain at the sound of the woman's cries.

Dinah looked through the office curtains. The woman's eyes were purple and blue from exhaustion, she was sweating. Dinah knew the woman's family had died the week before.

"I'm sorry, I am trying to help, but—" Levi's voice faltered. He drummed his skeletal fingers on his desk, his right eye twitching.

"Why won't you won't even *try* to help us?" the woman shouted up at them.

"If I let them in here—" he said to Dinah, and then stopped and straightened all the quills on his desk "Then . . . then . . ."

"I'm going home," Dinah said with finality.

"What?" Levi looked up at her shocked.

Dinah saw the fear in his eyes. He was barely a shadow of the brother she had known as a child. She remembered riding on his broad, strong shoulders as they ran around the yard outside their house. She remembered his hiccuping laughter dancing above the laughter of her eleven older brothers.

Her voice softened slightly. "Levi, I love you. And I'm not going to tell you what to do. But I can't stay here. I won't spend my days keeping sick people out of a doctor's office."

Levi sat at his desk, thinking for a long time. Then his face hardened as if he had landed on a decision. "You're right," He said, trying to keep his voice from cracking.

Leviticus swallowed hard. "Just give me a moment to write a letter to mom and dad."

He took out a fresh scroll and began writing. He wrote about how Adina and Merari had died and how grateful he was that they had sent Dinah to visit him. Then he paused. He thought of his brothers and his baby brother Joseph, whom he had never met.

Levi pulled out a second scroll and began to write down all his rules. The words poured out one after another. All his treatments. How everything was to be washed. Which herbs were effective and which were worthless folk remedies. It was late in the afternoon by the time he had compiled them all. He smiled, looking down at the long scroll. He had repeated himself more than he meant to, but it was good enough.

"I want you to deliver this for me." he said, handing her the two scrolls. The first one was marked for Jacob and Leah; the second was labeled the Scroll of Leviticus.

"You are quite good with a sword and you know how to keep yourself healthy," Leviticus said, forcing each word out of his mouth with a detached calm. "On your journey home I would ask that you stop in each village and speak with their elders. Explain to them how we treat people here. Then find someone who can read and make a copy of this scroll to remain with that village."

Levi said forcefully, "And make sure you wash before you leave each village so you don't bring the sickness with you to the next village. And when you finally get home to mom and dad I want you to give them a hug from me. After you've washed," Levi smiled.

"Come home with me," Dinah asked. Dinah looked her brother's tired eyes draped with purple and green, his skin pale and his hands red and cracked from washing. "Come home," she pleaded.

Leviticus shook his head. "My place is here." He smiled and tears gathered in the corners of his eyes. "And I'll see you when you come back." He added.

Dinah took the scrolls and left. Leviticus watched her from his office window as she quickly packed a bag of clean clothes and mounted her camel. "Make sure you always check the animals' organs and drain the blood—" he shouted down at her.

"And cook the meat myself, I remember," Dinah said, lifting up the scrolls before putting them in a leather satchel. She mounted her camel and clicked her tongue, and the camel trotted down the road past the villagers lining the fence. Levi thought she looked quite like a soldier riding into battle.

Levi sat at his desk and took out a quill and a fresh scroll.

> Dear Dinah,
>
> When you find me, I will likely be dead. I'm sorry to have sent you away but you were right. I'm a doctor and I can't just sit by watching my patients dying outside my door. I am so proud of you and I know you will have done your best to save as many lives as possible.
>
> And if you are not my sister Dinah and you find this letter, I want to make it perfectly clear that I chose to break my own rules in order to help my patients.
>
> As per the scrolls on the wall, they are a history of our village and the basis for my rules. You are free to read them. You may make copies of them, I believe they will be of value in helping to keep your community healthy.
>
> Shalom,
> Doctor Leviticus

Leviticus put down his quill, took a deep breath, opened the office door, and for the first time in weeks he stepped outside. "I will see the first patient now!" he shouted.

*"Who am I that I should go to Pharaoh, and bring the Israel-
ites out of Egypt?"*

—EXODUS 3:11

Aaron and the Burning Bush

"How did you find me?" Moses asked, warming his toes by the fire. The bitter mountain wind blew sparks off the rocky ledge.

"We told our spies to keep an eye out for a Hebrew trying not to act like an Egyptian Prince." Aaron smirked through his graying beard.

"Am I that obvious?" Moses laughed.

"Your clearly good enough to fool a Midianite."

Moses sat in a heavy silence across from his brother Aaron. Eight years had passed since he'd left Egypt. Eight years since he had seen his brother Aaron. He had left without knowing if he were still alive. And now they were warming their feet on the side of a mountain a month's ride from Egypt, in a forgotten corner of the desert.

Aaron stroked his graying beard, "You remarried."

"She's never left this valley," Moses paused, gesturing toward a small cluster of fires dotting the darkness. "When I met her she had never met a Hebrew." It was one of the things that Moses loved about his wife.

"Well, she picked a strange one to meet first."

"Maybe. I should have asked, why did you come find me?" Moses forced a smile and tossed another branch in the fire. The flames illuminated long scars on his brother Aaron's neck. The sight of the scars flooded Moses' mind with long suppressed memories—Aaron tied to a post, a fat Egyptian guard, Aaron wincing as the leather whip tore his back until his brown skin was soaked in blood.

Moses remembered sweating through his black Egyptian wig and white palace robe as he stood shoulder to shoulder with a crowd of enslaved Hebrews who were caked in mud. He remembered forcing his face to remain impassive as the fat Egyptian's white robes grew spotted with his brother's blood.

"Do something," his Hebrew mother had pleaded in his ear. "He's your brother."

Moses hadn't responded to her. Then Aaron fell to his knees. The Egyptian shouted at Aaron, "Stand up!"

But Aaron didn't respond. His brother's body was facedown and still. Moses was sure he was dead. "Stand up!" the Egyptian shouted, kicking Aaron in the ribs.

"Do something," his mother said between tears, her voice trembling. Moses felt sick, but he was determined to remain impassive.

The Egyptian kicked him again. "Stand up!"

"That's enough," Moses had said barely above a whisper.

His mother looked up at him. "Louder," she whispered.

"That's enough!" Moses shouted. At the sound of his voice, the other Egyptian guards knelt in supplication. But the fat Egyptian guard kept kicking Aaron's bloody body.

"I order you to stop," Moses shouted at him. He rushed toward the guard who kicked Aaron hard again. Moses felt rage surge through him. Before he knew what he was doing he had picked up a large rock and hit the guard over the head. He had swung hard, harder than he meant to. The stone broke through the guard's skull as if it were a ripe fruit.

Blood covered Moses' arm as he stood over the lifeless body of the Egyptian guard now lying next to his brother. Moses had never killed anything. He had never even butchered his own dinner. He had no idea how little it took to break open a skull. Moses looked up at the crowd. A thousand enslaved Hebrews stood silently shocked. The Egyptian guards still on their knees, watching Moses, waiting for an order.

The moment was hot and silent. Then Aaron coughed. Moses' mother ran to Aaron with her ear to his bloody mouth. Aaron whispered something to her. Moses' mother stood up and shouted. "He said, 'My brother Moses has returned to fight with us!'"

Moses felt his stomach turn in horror. It happened so quickly. The Hebrews overpowered the kneeling Egyptian guards with rocks and shovels. Moses watched as guards from across the pit descended from their towers to quell the uprising.

He dropped the bloody rock and ran. He ran across the pit, throwing off his wig and palace robe. In the chaos, he found a Hebrew robe and mounted a camel. He rode through the city and out the main gate, past the rolling green farms dotted with pigs and cows. Out of Egypt and into the endless desert. He rode until he didn't recognize the names of the small desert cities. Then he rode farther.

It had been eight harvests since he'd left Egypt. He had remarried, built a house, he had a son. He had a life in Midian. A life where he was a respected sheep herder—nothing less, nothing more.

Aaron stared into the fire awhile. When Aaron spoke his words were slow and labored.

"My baby boy was killed."

Moses didn't look up at his brother. "I'm sorry," Moses said to the fire. He felt the weight of old grief hanging in the silence between them.

"Elishe blames herself," Aaron said. "She was in labor for hours. Miriam had to hold a cloth over her mouth to muffle her screams. I had to leave to work in the pit—when I came home the Egyptian guards . . ." Aaron's voice faltered.

"You can stay here as long as you want," Moses said. "You can send for Elishe."

Aaron wiped his eyes. "I can't leave our people."

Moses felt an old anger flair at the accusation tucked into his brother's words. "That's what you think I've done," Moses shot back. As the words left his mouth he regretted them.

"I didn't say that," Aaron responded. His voice cold and flat.

Moses tried to swallow the anger, forcing his voice into a controlled directness. "After I killed that guard Pharaoh called for my arrest. He said he was going to kill me."

"You could have killed a hundred guards," Aaron scoffed. "What were they gonna do to the *son* of the princess?"

"Adopted son," Moses demanded.

"*Adopted* son," Aaron scoffed.

Moses stared into the fire, determined not to let his brother get the best of him. Moses had never told Aaron anything about his life in Pharaoh's palace, how he had grown up watching Egyptian mothers pull their kids away from him, always asking him if he was lost. They would tell him over and over that Hebrew kids weren't allowed in the Egyptian nursery.

How he watched those same mothers' faces change when they saw the princess hug him and ask, "Is there a problem here?"

He had never told Aaron how he was seated at the far end of the royal table. He watched his Egyptian sisters and brothers tell the Pharoah what they were studying in the royal academy, while Moses sat in silence, quietly picking the pig meat out of his dinner and feeding it to the dog that sat near his feet.

Sometimes Moses would steal a glance at the Hebrew girls who stood around the royal table holding large plates of grapes, beans, corns, and meats. They stood stone faced, like statues that could breathe. He never knew how to talk to Hebrew servants. The princess insisted Moses use the word "servant," not "*Hebrew* servant," and never "slave." In private, Moses sometimes tried to talk to the servants, asking them where they were from, whether they liked working in the palace. But the servants only ever responded with a cold politeness.

Moses spent most of his childhood alone in the palace full of people. Alone in the corner of the nursery or eating at the far end of the royal table. In his bedroom trying to learn to read, he'd work hard to keep the hieroglyphs from blurring and dancing across the scroll. An old Egyptian tutor sat next to him, scolding him as Moses tried to sound out each word.

Moses remembered sitting at his desk as his mother complained to his tutor that he wasn't keeping up with the other kids his age. Moses listened as his tutor carefully chose each of his next words. "Perhaps Hebrews aren't up to the rigor of school." Moses had never seen a Hebrew go to school, but he had assumed they went to their own schools. The idea that Hebrew children didn't go to school at all had never occurred to him.

"Hebrews are a nomadic people," the tutor explained to his mother. "They are built to work." Moses stared at the hieroglyphs of a children's story laying on his desk. He could barely read it. *Maybe he was built to work? Maybe they would get tired of trying to teach him and just send him to make bricks in the pit?* He waited for his mother to deny it, to say that *her* son was a prince and that it was the tutor's fault he couldn't read. But all he heard was his mother's footsteps as she walked away. The tutor was replaced the next day and Moses was never told why.

Shortly after, the princess began to regularly send Moses to visit his Hebrew family. The reason for these visits was not explained, but he soon grew to dread them. It was on his first visit that he met his brother Aaron. Their Hebrew mother had forced Aaron to stand at the door when Moses arrived. Moses looked at him. They were only a few years apart but their childhoods had shaped them into two very different bodies. Aaron was broad-shouldered and strong. His skin was sun-baked and his hands were large and rough. Not knowing any better, Moses asked his brother what he liked to do.

But it soon became clear that Aaron had never learned to read, never been to the theater, never eaten any of the foods that were served every night at the royal table. Their mother explained that Aaron had grown up making bricks in the pit. Moses tried to ask Aaron about it, but he was met with a cold politeness he recognized from the Hebrews in the palace. When they sat down for dinner at a small wooden table, their mother seated Moses at the head of the table. Aaron shot her a look that made Moses feel like he was used to sitting there. As soon as the meal was done, Aaron left with a group of Hebrew boys. Moses sat at the dinner table picking around the rotting vegetables on his plate. Baby Miriam stared at the stranger in their house as their mother fed her a brown mush.

For three days sick people "dropped by" and told their stories to the family. He soon realized that he was expected to do something for these people. His mother always reassured them, "Moses will tell the princess your story." Moses would nod along, trying to look sympathetic.

On the cold mountainside, Aaron tossed a branch in the fire and sparks flew up into the night sky. When he spoke it was with a measured calm. "Our sons have died. My own baby was murdered hours after he was born. And when our daughters grow up they live as slaves in the palace."

Moses winced as he heard his brother say "palace" with a clear derision.

"The tribal leaders have decided that it is time for us to leave."

"Leave?" Moses looked at his brother, confused. "Leave how?"

"Our men are too old to fight. Which is why I said that we must make the Egyptians lives *so miserable* that they let us go."

"Miserable enough that Ramses would let the entire empire collapse?"

Aaron's eyes flashed. "That's why we need you. You know how Ramses thinks. You understand how the empire works. You know where to push." Aaron used a long stick to push a log at the base of the fire. The collapsed logs were reduced to a smoldering pile of glowing embers, a cloud of sparks rose into the night wind . . .

Moses felt a pang of anger. He wanted to shout that he had never been allowed to go to the royal academy with Ramses. That he was never allowed to be an Egyptian child. But he took a deep breath and swallowed the thought. "I don't understand how everything in Egypt works," Moses said curtly.

"Egyptians give each of us one job. One." Aaron held his finger in the air. "We cook, we clean, we cut stones, I make bricks. And we do that one job until we collapse."

Moses' mind flashed with the image of Aaron's bloody body falling under the fat Egyptian guard's kicks. "That's because Pharaoh was always worried that if you—" Moses corrected himself, "If *the Hebrews* moved around too much, they would start getting ideas."

Aaron narrowed his eyes, but pushed past the slight. "Those are exactly the ideas that we need you to help us with."

Moses stared into the smoldering fire. The mountain wind blew cold and the flames leapt.

After a long time Aaron spoke, but this time his voice was softer. "I was never kind to you."

"You hated me," Moses shot back.

"Yes," Aaron smirked. "I hated you. I used to watch you pick the vegetables out of our dinner.

And I hated you—hated you for going to school and eating fresh vegetables every day."

"They hated me too," Moses said, looking into his brother's eyes.

Aaron's face softened. "There was a neighbor girl who served the royal dinner in the palace. She would stop by our house once in a while and tell us how you were doing. She told us they made you sit alone at the end of the table next to the dog."

"I used to feed the pig meat to that dog," Moses said, looking back at the fire as tears welled in his eyes.

"She told us that too," Aaron laughed. "Our mother was so proud of you."

Moses remembered that his mother always made a big show of seating him at the head of the table on his visits.

"We used to be a great people," Aaron said with a deep longing in his voice. "Noah built the largest boat the world had *ever seen*. He built that with his own two hands." Aaron's voice rose with passion. "Bab-el built a tower to the sky. Leviticus wrote a scroll that saved a thousand villages from the plague." Aaron threw his hands up in the dark, starry night. "And we have a chance right now to be remembered as the brothers who freed the Hebrews from slavery." Aaron looked at his brother. His eyes were pleading.

For a moment Moses imagined himself back in Egypt. Then his mind flashed with the sight of a mob of Hebrews descending on the kneeling Egyptian guards, watching the guards climb down from their towers with whips and clubs. He remembered dropping the stone and running.

Moses took a deep breath, "They'll kill us."

"They're already killing us," Aaron said. Moses felt his stomach clench painfully. He remembered his mother's voice whispering in his ear, "Do something. He's your brother."

Moses smoothed out the cold sand between them. Then he began to draw shapes with his finger. He drew a large triangle. "This is the palace," Moses said pointing at the triangle. Next to it he scooped out a handful of sand for the pit. Then he marked where the Hebrews lived, the sea, the Nile river running alongside the city. "This is the Nile, this is the pit, and this is where our people live. There are Hebrew servants stationed in every corner of the city and there is a secret river that flows under the city." Moses' finger connected the palace to the river. "We could try contaminating the water to the palace."

Aaron smiled wide at his brother. Then he looked down to study the map. "Some of the elders talked about growing locusts and releasing them into the Egyptian fields."

Moses raised his eyebrow suspiciously, "We would need *a lot* of locusts."

"We have a lot of people," Aaron said confidently, throwing a long branch into the fire.

The Pharoah said to them, "Moses and Aaron, why are you taking the people away from their work?"

—EXODUS 5:4

Moses and the Terrorist Attacks

Moses sat at the end of a long marble table inlaid with golden hieroglyphs and watched a Hebrew girl with long twisty brown hair hunched over a glistening roasted pig. She was slowly carving one piece at a time, placing the hot, pink meat onto the plates of the most powerful men in Egypt. The men spoke quietly to each other, each wearing a royal Egyptian robe and a shiny black wig. Every facet of life in Egypt was represented in the Egyptian nobility seated around the table. Except Pharoah. Pharaoh refused to sit down with Moses. But the nobility present showed Moses that Pharaoh was paying close attention to the Hebrew uprising.

Moses watched them eat, feeling naked in his simple slave robe, his own curly graying hair exposed. He had never been inside the palace without his royal robes and wig. The princess had forbidden it. As a child he was always scratching his itchy wig. Getting it twisted out of place. He remembered his mother bending down to straighten his wig, smiling at him. "You're a prince and princes must always look their best."

Moses watched as a royal messenger ran into the room. "The slaves have poisoned the milk," the messenger said, sweat beading on his forehead.

"Which milk," asked the head of Egyptian agriculture.

The messenger shook his head. "We don't know yet. Hundreds of Egyptian women and children have fallen sick. Thirty-seven are confirmed dead. Some people suspect the Hebrew nannies served Egyptian families poisoned milk and—"

The head of Egyptian agriculture stood up and ran out of the room. The messenger stopped speaking and ran after him, the clopping of their sandals echoing off the tall marble walls.

Moses sat stone-faced, trying not to conceal his surprise at the news. He didn't want the Egyptians to see a crack in the Hebrew leadership. He had told Aaron he didn't want anyone getting killed. He had told Aaron over and over. It was the *only* thing he had insisted on. But he swallowed his anger. He swallowed it like he had swallowed everything else.

Moses steepled his fingers over his mouth and watched the men react to the news. There was an immediate and undeniable shift in power. After Moses contaminated the Nile and released locusts into the Egyptians' fields, these men had only laughed at him. But now they shifted uncomfortably in their seats. No one looked at him. The Hebrew servant continued cutting slabs of meat from the roasted pig in the center of the silent table.

The head of the Egyptian army stood up and with murder in his eyes said, "I have to go home."

Another stood up and said, "I need to speak to Pharoah about this."

One by one the Egyptians left the table, until Moses was seated alone in the room with the Hebrew servant, who was still quietly carving the roasted pig.

That night Moses sat by the window inside his sister Miriam's small mud-walled house, Candles illuminated the faces of the twelve Hebrew elders from the twelve tribes of Israel. The air was thick with sweat and dust. The elders had bags under their eyes, their skin worn by the sun and the whip. They had been meeting late into the night for weeks and most of them were still working in the pit during the day. They hardly slept.

Moses sat at the end of the table, his hands steepled in a quiet anger, listening to what his brother Aaron was saying at the opposite end of the table.

"Their cows choked the nightshade down and Benjamin's men milked and fed half the city before the Egyptians even suspected us," Aaron shouted triumphantly, his forearms wrapped in bandages stained with blood and dirt.

"Our men counted—a quarter of the Egyptian herds are dead and half are sick and dying," Benjamin said. He was a broad-chested man who had put on muscle despite a diet of rice and water.

"Well done, Benjamin!" Aaron pounded his fist again.

"Stop moving so much," Miriam snapped at Aaron as she unwrapped the bandages and revealed the wounds of a whip deep in his forearms. Pharaoh had instructed the guards in the pit to "get the Hebrews under control." Aaron winced as Miriam began rewrapping his forearms with fresh cloth.

"Gershon, have your men found another way of contaminating the water?"

Doctor Gershon spoke slowly, his bald and eyebrowless skin clinging to his bones like a loosely wrapped sheet. "Our men found more red clay deposits, but Pharoah must have found them as well, because both sections are heavily guarded."

"Keep looking," Aaron said undeterred. "Miriam, how are we doing getting water to our people?"

"I reminded the mothers to boil the water before they let the children drink it. But it still tastes like dead frogs." She cut Aaron's bandages with her teeth.

"Well done, Miriam," Aaron smiled. "What's next?" he asked, looking at the map. Aaron's eye caught Moses'. Moses hands were steepled over his lips. He hadn't spoken during the entire meeting.

"Something on your mind, brother?" Aaron inquired patronizingly. "How are your *negotiations* going? I imagine Pharaoh wasn't laughing today."

Moses stared at his brother. He felt the elder's gaze rest on him. They had all agreed on contaminating the water and releasing the locusts, but he had not been told about poisoning children's milk. Aaron and the elders had planned it behind his back.

"The Egyptians are rattled," Moses said. "Pharaoh sent word that he is willing to channel fresh water into all the Hebrew neighborhoods."

There was a long silence. Then Aaron burst out laughing. The other elders looked up at him and then joined in. Moses was unprepared for this. He fumed silently, his fingers still steepled over his lips.

"You have been negotiating for a week and you got him to *dig a channel*?" Aaron asked sarcastically.

"It's a start." Moses slammed his fist down in disgust at their laughter.

"A start?" Aaron shouted louder. The small room fell silent.

"Benjamin? When Pharaoh decided he wanted fresh water in his summer palace, did you ever *once* see an Egyptian digging alongside you?" Aaron asked, smirking.

Benjamin narrowed his gaze on Moses, "Not once."

"Hundreds of *children* died from that milk," Moses said, unable to hold back his anger.

"*Egyptian* children," Miriam corrected him.

"What choice did those children have in all of this?" Moses snapped back at her.

"Choice?" Aaron asked with derision, his finger pointing the accusation at his brother. "We never had any choices. Moses, *you* are the only person at this table who has ever had any *choices*. They murdered our sons. They forced our daughters to breastfeed their babies. When we stopped for a drink, they whipped us until our backs are too raw to sleep. We have never had *any*—"

They were interrupted by three hard knocks on the front door. It was the signal that Egyptian soldiers were coming down the street. Miriam quickly blew out the candles. The room plunged into a dark heavy silence.

Moses could hear Egyptians shouting outside. Then a woman shouted. "No, not my—. No!" she screamed. They were taking her baby. "No, please, please . . ." She sobbed. Moses felt his heart beating fast, his mouth went dry. Other Hebrews were shouting at the soldiers. "Murderers!" "Shame!" It was a long time before the shouting stopped. Then they heard three more knocks on the door.

Miriam lit the candles. Moses could see her eyes were wet with tears. "Moses, *why* are you defending them!" Miriam whispered loudly. He could hear a deep well of anger rising in her voice. "They killed my baby. He was your nephew!"

Moses couldn't meet her eyes. Moses felt his stomach twist. He steepled his hands over his own wet eyes. He felt sick and tired and he wanted to go back to the desert. To go back to being a no one from nowhere, herding his sheep, sleeping beside his wife, their son gently snoring beside them.

Doctor Gershon, his raspy withered voice hardly louder than a whisper, "Moses. Your heart is soft. Maybe being raised in the palace . . ." he trailed off. "You knew these Egyptians as children and mothers," Doctor Gershon pulled back his sleeve revealing a criss-cross of scars covering his arm. ". . . but you never knew them as masters." The elders nodded in solemn agreement.

Doctor Gershon continued quietly, "If killing is what it takes, then that is what it takes." The doctor rubbed his bald temple as if it pained him to say it. The rest of the elders nodded in solemn agreement.

"Then how are we any better than they are?'" Moses asked.

Aaron leaned over the map of Egypt and shook his head, "Moses, that's what you don't seem to understand. This isn't about being *better*. This is about being *free*." There was a silence and then

Aaron continued. "Tonight we move forward with the plan to kill all the firstborn sons of Egypt."

Moses stared at his brother in disbelief. "You can't . . ." He couldn't believe what he was hearing.

"We can't wait for the Egyptians to regroup." Aaron cut him off. "Doctor Gershom is right. If killing a hundred children only gets us a ditch, than they are more stubborn than we expected."

"Let me . . ." Moses said trying to frantically come up with a way to stall. "Let me . . . Let me talk with the Queen. Maybe I can convince her." Moses felt the air leaving the room. He suddenly felt small and stupid. He'd felt this way on his childhood visits to Aaron and Miriam's, reluctanly seated at the head of the table as Hebrews stared at him like a curiosity.

Benjamin smirked. "Don't worry, Moses, we aren't planning on killing *all* the Egyptians' baby boys." The elders laughed uncomfortably. Moses stood up with his fist clenched.

"Now now, Benjamin, my brother didn't put himself in that basket." The elders chuckled. "And we shouldn't fault him for holding out some hope. Who knows?" Aaron threw his bandaged arms in the air. "Maybe he can convince his dear old mom."

Moses left the house and felt the cold night surround him. The stagnant air reeked of rot and defecation. The mother whose child had been taken was sobbing in her illuminated bedroom across the street. Grieving neighbors were gathered outside the small home built of broken bricks and rotting timbers.

He mounted a camel and rode through the dark, empty Hebrew neighborhood. At the end of the street was a large channel that separated the Hebrew and Egyptian neighborhoods. He stopped at the Egyptian guard's station located on the divide between. A small bridge connected these two parts of the city. A soldier in full armor stood at the gate. Moses handed the guard a piece of papyrus with the royal seal on it.

"So you're the Moses people keep talking about," the Egyptian guard scoffed.

"I am," Moses said.

The Egyptian soldier narrowed his eyes in contempt. "My nephew died from that milk you poisoned." The Egyptian looked at him with murder in his eyes, his hand on his sword. Moses pulled the camel's reigns tight. "And if I was Pharoah I would gut you like a fish and hang your carcass from this bridge." Then the soldier spit at Moses. Moses felt the wet spit run down his leg, but he didn't move. They stood for a moment in silence before the soldier waved him through the gate.

He rode across the wooden bridge. On the other side, the Egyptian street was lined with two- and three-story houses painted white. Outside the houses the yards were dotted with trees and small statues. He could see Egyptian families inside getting ready for bed. He rode through a dozen streets, the houses getting larger and larger as he neared the riverside palace.

He finally slowed his camel in the moon-lit shadow of Pharoah's brick and marble palace. A guard stood near a small unpolished wooden door on the side of the palace wall. Moses had never entered the palace through the slaves' entrance, but he was afraid to use the main palace doors tonight. A Hebrew woman emerged from the door. She carried a bucket of piss and feces and dumped the filth into the black waters of the Nile. Moses watched it flow downstream into the Hebrew neighborhoods. In the morning the shores would be lined with Hebrew mothers bathing their children and filling up water jars for breakfast.

The woman disappeared back through the door. He showed his papyrus to the guard and entered a warm hallway illuminated by candles and smelling of smoke and sweat. Young Hebrew women were bustling up and down a long dark set of stairs, their arm fulls of firewood.

As he walked he realized he had no memories associated with these halls. His mother had forbidden him from coming down here with "the servants." He walked down a long stretch of hallway and saw a room with a dozen Hebrew women breastfeeding Egyptian babies.

He continued on, checking the walls for the servants' entrance to the royal hall. The hallway opened into a large room with pots and jars. A Hebrew woman in a stained apron was chopping garlic, the small clicking of the blade was the only sound in the room.

Moses had the strange feeling of being lost in his childhood home. "Excuse me, where is the door to the royal hall?"

"Who wants to know?" the Hebrew woman asked, not looking up. There was a large pile of cloves stacked into a pyramid on the wooden counter.

"Moses," he paused uncomfortably. "I'm here to meet with the Queen."

"Are you Miriam's brother Moses?" she looked up and pointed at him with her knife.

"Yes," he said, taking a step back.

"You owe me two nights sleep."

"What?" Moses asked confused.

"That stunt turned the river red. I was piling dead frogs up and down the river for two sleepless nights." Her voice was cold, "But I bet you didn't talk about who was going to have to clean up that shit, did you? No. Just a bunch of boys playing war. Thought you would stick it to them," she said stabbing the air.

"And now Pharaoh's demanding fresh milk on his table for breakfast in the morning. So I had to send my thirteen-year-old daughter out into the desert at night to find a jar of milk you idiots hadn't poisoned!" She shouted at him. "And if she gets . . ." she paused, wiping tears from her eyes. "If something happens to her on the road tonight you'd better check your milk."

Moses stood in the doorway feeling small and foolish, wondering how many Hebrews thought of him as "playing at war." He looked at the massive pile of garlic she still had to chop while she worried that her daughter was out on the road at night.

"I'm sorry," he said. He wanted to say something more but she grabbed another garlic clove and began chopping. The click of the blade on the table once again filling the room. Tears rolled down her cheeks.

"The door to the royal hall is right behind you," she said, not looking up.

He stood for a moment watching her work. But after a moment it was clear she was done with him. Moses turned and stood in front of the small wooden door and took a deep breath. Then he stepped into a massive room bathed in gold and light.

The room was filled with the smell of his mother's rose and lemongrass incense. The light from large torches reflected off tall golden pillars and walls engraved with dazzling blue hieroglyphs.

Moses looked up at the blue outline of the ancient Pharaoh wearing two golden crowns. He remembered his tutor walking him around the royal hall. "This is King Menes. He wears two crowns because he united the two kingdoms of Egypt," his tutor explained.

"The Hebrews and the Egyptians?" Moses asked.

"No!" The tutor slapped him hard on the back of the head. "We *talked* about this in your lesson this morning. King Menes united the northern and southern kingdoms of *Egypt.*"

His mother's fragile voice cut through his memory. "You always loved those pictures."

Moses turned and saw his mother walking down the long stairs at the far end of the room.

"I didn't recognize you at first. I wasn't expecting you to come out of the servants' door." She smiled, leaning heavily on her cane. His mother wore the same bright painted red lips and white cheeks. But her lips were now cracked and the white make-up only highlighted the deep wrinkles in her cheeks. She looked much older, much more frail than when Moses had last seen her eight years ago.

She looked Moses up and down. And Moses felt ashamed to be seen by her in only his Hebrew robe, his curly graying hair exposed.

"Let me get you something to wear. Milcah!" she clapped and her large golden bracelets jingled.

"No, Mother, I'm fine," Moses tried to assure her, and reassure himself.

Milcah was the servant who had been chopping garlic. She entered the room carrying a golden chalice smelling of garlic.

The Queen took a long drink. "Garlic is good for old skin," she winked at Moses.

"Milcah, please bring my son some clothes." His mother brushed some sand out of Moses' hair. "And some fresh hair as well." Milcah bowed.

Moses felt small, this wasn't the way he wanted this to go. "Wait. Milcah you don't have to bring me any clothes." But Milcah didn't acknowledge his command and she left the room.

"Why don't you want any clothes?" The Queen waved her hand dismissively. "Oh, I get it." She looked him up and down and rolled the rough fabric of Moses' robe between her fingers. "This is all a part of your whole *thing* now." Moses felt a pang of shame in his stomach.

The Queen stepped back and looked at him as if he was a rebellious teenager, "You know what? Wear whatever you want." She adjusted her dark black wig, which was held in place by a band of gold with a large red jewel in the center. She smiled wide.

"Ramses told me you got married," her bright voice restarting the conversation.

"He what?" Moses was caught off-guard. He had been in the palace a dozen times and hadn't seen his mother. He had assumed it was because she was ashamed of him, but she seemed unphased by her son leading the Hebrew uprising.

"He told me you got married to a farmer's daughter in Midian, but that you didn't want all the pomp that would go along with all of us showing up." The Queen nodded knowingly. Moses was stunned. Ramses had found him in Midian. And he had just left him alone.

"Did your wife enjoy the bracelet I sent her?" The Queen rolled one of the gold bracelets still on her wrist.

"She loved it," Moses lied, his mind still reeling from all this new information.

"What is she like? I always envisioned you with a quiet type."

Moses felt like he was sinking into his old life. Alone with his mother in the palace trying to pretend that things weren't the way they were. Trying to pretend it was normal that the Egyptian princess had adopted a Hebrew baby, a baby that her father had sentenced to death.

Moses tried to swallow all this, to push it out of his mind and focus on the words she was saying. His mother was asking about his wife. He realized it was the first time *anyone* had asked about her.

"Zipporah isn't quiet," he smiled. "She loves making big meals and inviting the whole village over. When I first saw her, she was telling jokes to all the women at the well. They were rolling with laughter. I asked her for a drink and she handed me the bucket and told me to get my own drink." Moses laughed at the memory.

"Did you tell her you were a prince?" the Queen leaned closer.

"No," Moses sighed. "I never told her. She just married me."

"I bet she was surprised when you gave her the royal bracelet from the Queen of Egypt?" the Queen laughed.

Moses had forgotten about her bracelet. He felt the joy of the moment wither inside him as he looked at the floor and tried to knit the lie back into his story.

"She loved it," he said. "I told her it was a family heirloom from my mother."

The Queen smiled and rubbed his back. "I'm so glad to hear that. Send her my love."

Milcah re-entered the room. She walked in front of Moses and held out a bright white robe, a black wig, and polished leather sandals. Her face was placid and calm. She looked down at his feet as if they had never met.

"I don't want this," Moses said, irritated and embarrassed.

Milcah didn't move.

"Just put it over there. Thank you," the Queen said, pointing behind Moses. "Okay, so what is so important that you *finally* want to talk to me."

"I'm sorry. But I didn't know how you were going to take all this."

She took another long drink from the chalice. "Well, I was worried that you had fallen in with those Hebrew terrorists. Did you hear about that nanny that poisoned the milk and fed to the child? The child she was caring for!" She exclaimed.

"It makes me sick to think about. Can you imagine?" she put her hand on her heart. "It's just terrible. But Ramses assured me that you weren't a part of it."

"*Ramses* said that?" Moses said before he could stop himself.

"All this nonsense about Hebrews polluting the water and poisoning farmer's kids. He told me you weren't a part of it." She put her hand on his shoulder. "And I was so relieved. I didn't raise you like that. I understand why people were ready to believe it. Because of that nasty rumor after you left. Did you hear? People were saying you killed a guard outside the pit." She took another long drink out of the chalice.

Moses couldn't find words. He had stood in this room for the last two weeks and called Ramses "a baby murderer." He had told his nobleman to "let our people go or the blood of Egyptians would be on his head." But Ramses had kept all this from their mother and protected her from seeing her two beloved sons fighting. Moses had never felt love for his brother Ramses, but he now felt ashamed of himself. Moses felt tears rolling down his cheeks.

"Is everything alright?" his mother's voice sounded full of compassion. "Even as a little boy you always took it so hard when people said mean things about you."

He remembered why he had come to meet her. To tell her she had to convince Ramses to let the Hebrews go. That more kids were going to die. But Moses looked at his mother's compassionate face and he couldn't bring himself to say it. His brother had left her out of it. And Moses was grateful to him.

He wiped his eyes and tried to regain his composure. He knew this was the last time he would see his mother, the woman who had done her best to love him in her way. He wanted to spend one last evening with her. So he sat down on the wooden chair next to her and asked the question he had waited his whole life to ask. "Why did you pull me out of that river?"

His mother smiled as she sat down on a polished wooden chair. "Well, I was a very impulsive fifteen-year-old. And I saw you crying and I picked you up. And I said I was adopting you. And I was the princess of Egypt—who could tell me no?" She let out a deep self-effacing laugh. It was this laugh that had always made the Egyptian people love her. "Well, let me tell you. My father—the Pharaoh of Egypt mind you—was so upset. 'We can't have a Hebrew running around the palace,' he said. But I told him there was no way I was going to put you back in the river." She smiled.

"Did you know they were *killing* the Hebrew boys?" the words flew out of Moses's mouth. His mother sighed deeply. "No. No, I didn't. I was just a young girl and father didn't think it was appropriate to talk about the population crisis."

"Population crisis?" Moses' eyebrows narrowed.

"There wasn't enough food to feed everyone. The boys were being put out of their misery before they starved. That's why I always sent you with a bag of grain when you visited your birth family."

Moses was dumbfounded. He knew his childhood had been marked by unprecedented rainfall and crop yields. He remembered Egyptian farmers joking about how they didn't have enough people to bring in the harvest. He looked at her, almost unwilling to believe that his mother had just believed everything she had ever been told. He was torn between a desire to shout at her and go on protecting her.

But he had one more question he wanted to ask. "Why *did* you send me back to visit my Hebrew family?"

She put her frail white hand on his painted white cheek and sighed, "I hated that my family treated you badly. Made you sit at the end of the table, wouldn't let you go to school, always called you names. And I just thought that if you saw the life you avoided, that you would be grateful for the things you did have—" She stopped as her black eyeliner streaked with tears slowly falling along the creases in her face. "It wasn't my best moment." She wiped her eyes, smearing the white paint and eyeliner together.

He forced a smile. "You did the best you could, mom." He patted her thigh. "You saved me from the river, and that was more than most people would have done."

"I tried," his mother nodded and rested her head on his shoulder.

He put his arm around her and they sat in the thick royal air, smelling of garlic and lemongrass and rosewater, listening to the sound of torches crackling. He felt her wig still itchy against his neck. Sitting alone with his mother had always been the happiest moments of his childhood.

When he sensed the sadness had passed, he squeezed her shoulder reassuringly.

"I have to go, but thank you for this. It was so good to talk."

The Queen stood up and hugged him. "Anytime. Anytime."

"I hope to see you again soon."

Moses said and he turned to leave the main hall through the servants' door. He walked past the now-empty room filled with jars, past the empty nursing room, and out of the palace. It was a cold quiet night, the moon still bright enough to cast a shadow.

Moses stared out at the black Nile river and suddenly the weight of all the death and lies overwhelmed him. He thought of the nannies that had fed their master's children poison. He thought of Aaron's son. The nephew who had been killed before his father had even seen him. The old men who stumbled in the pit and never come home. His mother believing it was all just merciful population control.

Moses felt his breath tighten as if the enormity of the pain pushed down on his chest. He got down on his knees and the ground seemed to tilt and spin under him. He felt his stomach lurch and he threw up into the sand. He rolled onto his back and felt the cold wet ground on his neck. He could taste blood in his vomit. His mind flashed with the broken skull of the Egyptian guard. He heard Aaron's voice in his mind. *You're the only one who's ever had choices.*

What do I do now? He thought. He had tried to run away. He had tried to make peace. He had tried to keep anyone from getting killed. But none of it had mattered. His nephew was still dead and by morning all the Egyptian firstborn sons would also be dead. He should have told his mother to hide her grandchildren. He cursed himself for forgetting.

The he saw a head lean over him, blocking out the moon.

"Do you need help?" a Hebrew teenager asked. Her hair was wrapped, with a single curl falling loose. She had a jar of milk and a sack of flour in her arms.

"Are you Milcah's daughter?" Moses asked, wiping the blood from his lip. She nodded.

"Good," he sighed, a wave of relief rolling over him. "Your mother is inside and she's worried about you."

Moses watched her disappear through the servants' door. He thought of her mother nervously chopping garlic, waiting for her daughter to come home. He thought of the sobs of the Hebrew woman whose child had been stolen that night. He thought of all the Egyptian mothers holding the lifeless bodies of their sons. Milcah's words "boys playing war" echoed in his mind.

Moses made up his mind. He pushed himself back to his feet and mounted his camel. He rode quickly through the dark Egyptian neighborhoods without stopping until he was at the gate to Miriam's yard. As he tied up the camel he could see a fire crackling behind the fence. Inside the house Miriam was rolling out bread dough.

Moses picked a large rock and opened the wooden gate.

Aaron was seated near the fire. Benjamin stood behind him, his hand resting on his sword hilt.

"What did she say?" Aaron asked, warming his bare feet around a pile of embers.

Moses rolled the rock around in his hands. "She wasn't there."

"That's disappointing. But expected," Aaron said, leaning closer to the embers. Aaron motioned to Benjamin, "Tell them we are still moving forward."

"Before you do this, I want to ask you to reconsider." Moses said as he rolled the rock in his hands. It felt heavy and solid. He had been so young last time. But in Midian he had learned to butcher, learned the value of taking a life quickly and painlessly. He knew how hard to swing.

Aaron shook his head. "Moses, how many Hebrew boys were killed by Egyptians today."

Moses stared into the fire. He didn't know.

"Benjamin, how many?"

"Seventeen baby boys, eight men were beaten to death after fighting a guard in the pit," he paused. "And two grandfathers died."

"Twenty-seven of our brothers died at the hands of the Egyptians today." Aaron bared his teeth. Moses remembered seeing Aaron tied to the pole all those years ago. He remembered feeling the Egyptian's skull give way under the weight of Moses' rock.

"Why the firstborn sons?" Moses asked.

"Ah, now there's the right question." Aaron smirked. "I got the idea from when I was a boy. I was working in the garden of a wealthy Egyptian family. The family loved each other and they treated me as well any Egyptian treats us. But one day the oldest brother fell sick, and all day I watched as his brothers waited on his every need. They were falling all over each other to help him. But despite everything, he died the next morning. And while their mother is still sobbing over her firstborn's body, the brothers turned on each other, dividing up his firstborn inheritance like thieves. Shouting about who gets the house, who gets the farm, who got his seat on the council. I stood there all morning just watching them fight," Aaron laughed. "I didn't do a lick of work all day. And then finally I just went home. And no one even noticed I was gone."

Moses stared into the fire, feeling the weight of the rock in his hands. He remembered looking down at the dead Egyptian. His skull crushed. Blood soaking into the sandy ground. He remembered seeing Aaron's back raw from the whip.

"Where will you take everyone?" Moses asked.

"Midian seemed nice," Aaron said.

"The Midians live there," Moses said.

"They'll make room,"

"And if they don't?" Moses looked at his brother.

"I didn't see anything we couldn't handle."

Moses thought about Zipporah's family in Midian. They wouldn't stand for their land being overrun by Hebrews. He imagined his in-laws gathering their friends and neighbors together. The Midians would fight, and they would lose.

"Midian isn't big enough for all of us," Moses lied.

"Us?" Aaron raised his eyebrow smiling. "You've decided to come with us?"

"We could go to the land of our ancestors. Back to Canaan," Moses said, drawing in the sand between them. The fire illuminated the lines and circles. He drew the Red Sea, the mountain of Sinai, and the long desert dotted with oases.

"There is a desert between Egypt and Canaan. It is a long and grueling journey, but I have seen maps in the palace that show where the oases are." Moses lied again as his finger wound its way through the map he had just made up.

Aaron leaned over to examine the map in the sand. Moses' stomach twisted as he envisioned his brother's skull collapsing, blood flowing over his hands. His mind flashed with the broken skull of the guard.

Aaron looked up at Moses and they made a long, hard eye contact. "You can put the rock down brother," Aaron said. "It won't do any good."

Moses tried to soften his facial expression. He loosened his tight grip on the rock. "I was just warming my hands," Moses tried to say casually.

"There is no need for lies, brother," Aaron said, putting his hand on Moses' shoulder. His arm was wrapped in browning bandages. "I know that look. I have seen it on my master's faces for forty years. It's the look of someone who is deciding how hard to hit me."

Moses dropped the rock and Aaron stood up. "And if I we are finally being honest, I should tell you that I gave the order to kill the firstborns right after you left the meeting tonight. The Egyptians will die and killing me won't change that." The flames danced on his hardened face. Aaron nodded at Benjamin.

Moses felt a burlap sack tighten over his head. He didn't struggle or shout. He watched the red glow of the fire through the gaps in the stretched fabric, the smell of flour filling his nose. Then he felt two cold iron chains heavy on his wrists.

"Moses, I need you to take us across this desert. I agree with you that we belong in Caanan, the land of our ancestors."

Moses felt the weight of the chains on his wrists. But then he felt his muscles relax. He let go of the rock and sat back in his chair. He was finally powerless to do anything except follow Aaron's commands. He felt the guilt of all the killings leaving him, there was no longer anything he could do.

He felt Benjamin's hands under his arm, pulling him to his feet. "We will remove the chains during the day. The people will need to see us as a united front."

"Don't tell Miriam." It was all Moses said through the burlap and the smell of flour.

"I won't tell her you tried to kill me," Aaron said. "If you don't try and run again."

Moses was pushed forward and his hands reached out in front of him. He felt the camel's hide.

Aaron whispered to Benjamin, "Take him out of town and wait for us by the sea. We will cross tomorrow at low tide."

He mounted the camel and felt it slowly walk down quiet streets. Through the burlap he could hear people whispering in Hebrew. He felt warm air pouring out of hot kitchen windows. The smell of bread in the oven filled the slim roads between tightly packed homes. The Hebrews were preparing to leave.

He was out of the city and into the Egyptian plantations when the first light of morning shone through the burlap fabric. The cold metal chains were a stark contrast to the sun now warming his arms. He heard cows crying out to be milked.

"Can you take this off me," Moses asked. "I want to see my home one last time."

He felt the sack rub against his beard as it was pulled off his head. Below him Benjamin was slowly walking, eating a piece of flatbread with one hand, holding the reins to the camel with the other. Moses wrists were chained to the camel's saddle. In front of him, hills of green farms were dotted with grazing pigs and cows. Beyond the farms lay nothing but sun-scorched sand as far as he could see.

"How about these?" Moses said jangling his chains.

Benjamin shrugged, "Aaron didn't give me the keys."

Then Moses heard the sound of cheering from behind him. He turned his head and saw morning sun illuminating the palace, the morning light blinding off the golden spires. The he saw people begin to pour out of the archway to the city.

Hebrew women and children dancing, spinning, and jumping. The Hebrews all wore long colorful Egyptian robes. Hebrew men were seated on Egyptian-style carriages, baskets and jars strapped to every side. Young men laughed as they haphazardly rounded up cows from the empty Egyptian farms along the main road. Moses smiled at the infectious joy. He had never seen his people allowed to celebrate in the streets.

Then he saw Miriam and Aaron standing atop a massive two-story high Egyptian caravan inlaid on all sides with golden hieroglyphs. Aaron looked like a king, wearing a long Egyptian military robe and a golden crown on his head. Miriam stood beside him like a queen dressed in Egyptian royal garb. They were shouting with joy and tossing golden coins to the crowd of Hebrew children that were running along the parade.

For the first time in his life Moses saw all his people dressed in riches and marching in freedom. The sight brought tears to his eyes.

Miriam raised a ram's horn to her mouth and blew it long and clear. The shouting stopped and all eyes turned to the woman standing on top of the tallest caravan in the parade.

Miriam's voice sang out the first verse of the song of the Hebrew people.

"*Adam slayed the snake with a flaming torch,*" she sang clear as the blue sky.

"*As Cain bandaged his brother's wounds,*" a great chorus of Hebrew voices sang back.

"*Noah built his family an ark,*" Miriam sang.

"*As Naameh healed her neighbors,*" the chorus swelled with more voices.

"*Leviticus remained clean.*"

All of the bald and eyebrowless descendants of Levi raised their voices, "*And saved the desert from the plague.*" Everyone cheered for the doctors and nurses of their people.

Miriam then blew the horn again and her clear unwavering voice sang a new verse for a new day.

"*Aaron told Pharoah to let my people go.*" They cheered wildly for their hero. And Aaron nodded raising his fist in triumph.

"*But Pharoah said no, so we turned the water red and the milk sour.*" Miriam sang and the crowd cheered.

"*Aaron told Pharoah to let my people go. But Pharoah said no, so we took the gold and left,*" Miriam sang as she shouted in joy and tossed gold coins into the air.

The crowd took up the song from there. They sang the new song over and over as they danced into the endless desert.

www.ingramcontent.com/pod-product-compliance
Lightning Source LLC
Chambersburg PA
CBHW050410030726
47503CB00006B/2120

* 9 7 8 1 5 3 2 6 8 2 2 8 5 *